THE FORTUNES OF TEXAS

*Follow the lives and loves of a complex family
with a rich history and deep ties
in the Lone Star State*

SECRETS OF FORTUNE'S GOLD RANCH

Welcome to Fortune's Gold Ranch...where the vistas of Emerald Ridge are as expansive as the romantic entanglements that beckon its visitors!

TO CATCH A FORTUNE

World traveler and oilman Jonathan Porter never expected to put down roots in Texas ranch country—as a father, no less! It's just Jonathan's luck to tangle with local royalty Vivienne Fortune as he grapples with parenting the son he'd never known existed. But when Vivienne needs his help to fight a family foe, the duo's sparring starts to look a lot like love!

Dear Reader,

Vivienne Fortune has worked hard to become the forewoman of Fortune's Gold Ranch, and with the added responsibility, she has sworn off men—some who regard her as their "sugar mama."

When wealthy oil heir Jonathan Porter confronts her with tangible evidence that someone from her ranch has stolen a Porter family heirloom, she vehemently denies any of her employees could be responsible for the crime because the Fortune ranch has also been victimized by a number of thefts. Despite his accusation, Vivienne finds herself drawn to the handsome international oilman—and shocked to discover that he has a baby boy.

Meanwhile, Jonathan is faced with the dilemma of caring for one-year-old Daniel, the son he hadn't known existed. Jonathan finds fatherhood more challenging than anything he has ever experienced. He's grateful for Vivienne's support when it comes to Daniel, but he also believes he's becoming much too dependent on her not only for himself but also his son. What he has to ask himself is if Vivienne is who he needs to make his family complete.

I hope you'll enjoy Vivienne and Jonathan's story as they discover not only each other but also what it means to become team Fortune and Porter.

Happy reading,

Rochelle Alers

TO CATCH A FORTUNE

ROCHELLE ALERS

THE FORTUNES OF TEXAS

Special thanks and acknowledgment are given to
Rochelle Alers for her contribution to
The Fortunes of Texas: Secrets of Fortune's Gold Ranch miniseries.

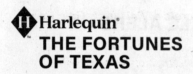

**THE FORTUNES
OF TEXAS**

Recycling programs
for this product may
not exist in your area.

ISBN-13: 978-1-335-99682-4

To Catch a Fortune

Copyright © 2025 by Harlequin Enterprises ULC

Harlequin Enterprises ULC
22 Adelaide St. West, 41st Floor
Toronto, Ontario M5H 4E3, Canada
www.Harlequin.com

Printed in Lithuania

MIX
Paper | Supporting
responsible forestry
FSC® C021394

Since 1988, nationally bestselling author **Rochelle Alers** has written more than eighty books and short stories. She has earned numerous honors, including the Zora Neale Hurston Award, the Vivian Stephens Award for Excellence in Romance Writing and a Career Achievement Award from *RT Book Reviews*. She is a member of Zeta Phi Beta Sorority, Inc., Iota Theta Zeta Chapter. A full-time writer, she lives in a charming hamlet on Long Island. Rochelle can be contacted through her website, rochellealers.org.

Books by Rochelle Alers

Harlequin Special Edition

The Fortunes of Texas: Secrets of Fortune's Gold Ranch

To Catch a Fortune

Montana Mavericks: The Anniversary Gift

The Maverick's Thirty-Day Marriage

Bainbridge House

A New Foundation
Christmas at the Château

Montana Mavericks: Brothers & Broncos

Thankful for the Maverick

Furever Yours

The Bookshop Rescue

Wickham Falls Weddings

Home to Wickham Falls
Her Wickham Falls SEAL
The Sheriff of Wickham Falls
Dealmaker, Heartbreaker

Visit the Author Profile page
at Harlequin.com for more titles.

Chapter One

Jonathan, you have an eleven-month old baby boy, and I need you to return to the States as soon as possible.

Jonathan Porter had thought the attorney who headed the legal department of Porter Oil was pranking him when he'd answered his phone the night before. He didn't tell the man he'd known for certain that there was no way he could have fathered a child that age because he had been dividing his time between Texas and the Middle East, growing Porter Oil International with his father. And furthermore, he hadn't been involved with any woman during that time.

The last relationship he'd had had fizzled once he'd told the woman—who had hinted that she wanted an engagement ring after three months of dating—that he hadn't been ready for a commitment, and they'd needed more time to be together given his hectic travel schedule. Then she'd wanted him to purchase for her birthday a bag with a hefty five-figure price tag—and that's when he told her he was flat broke, and as the family's black sheep he was living paycheck to paycheck. It was only after he'd paid rent and a car note that there was very little left over for the designer handbag.

It had become a test because Jonathan had believed women were only interested in him because of his family's connections. Danielle Matthews failed the test, and she had also broken his heart once he realized he was falling in love with her. She'd stopped taking his phone calls and after several weeks he knew what they'd had was over. She'd walked out on him and when he'd left the States for Dubai several months later, he'd vowed to forget her.

Jonathan closed his eyes, attempting to get some sleep during the fifteen-hour flight from Dubai to Texas. The notion that he has fathered a child nagged at him like raw wound. Although he and Danielle hadn't made it as a couple, if she had been pregnant, and refused to marry him, there was no doubt he would have provided child support and agreed to co-parent. And not being in his child's life would have been nonnegotiable. Not for Jonathan, because Porters were almost fanatical when it came to family.

He did manage to get five hours of uninterrupted sleep by the time the Porter corporate jet touched down at the Dallas Fort Worth International Airport, where one of Porter Oil's drivers was awaiting his arrival. After clearing customs, Jonathan nodded to the man holding open the rear door of the town car for him.

"Welcome home, Mr. Porter."

Jonathan smiled and nodded. "Thank you. It feels good to be back." He'd always looked forward to being in the States because he enjoyed being with his family.

"Where to, Mr. Porter?" the driver asked, reaching for Jonathan's carry-on.

"You can drop me off at my house in Emerald Ridge. You don't have to wait for me because I'll drive myself to the office," he said, ducking his head and slipping onto the rear seat. He'd planned to shower and change clothes before meeting the lawyer at the Emerald Ridge office building, where Porter Oil occupied an entire floor in the large, ornate limestone structure.

What he really wanted was to get into bed and sleep, and then not do much else until his body reacclimated to the central time zone.

However, that wasn't going to happen today because he was anxious to meet with the head of the company's legal department to straighten out what Jonathan had begun to think that maybe it could be a trumped-up paternity scam. Yes, he had slept with women, yet not so many he couldn't remember their names or faces, and there had never been a time when he hadn't used protection. Now, he would have to put off kicking back and readjusting to being home for at least another day until he straightened everything out.

Returning to the States had come at a good time because he was anxious to not only reunite with his mother, aunts, and grandparents, but also his sister, Imani, who had made him an uncle for the first time when she'd given birth to a son the year before. He'd had several Zoom calls with his sister because of the nine-hour time difference and that's when she'd brought him up to speed on what was going on back home.

Apparently, there'd been a series of thefts and sabotages at three area ranches, and although the thief had been apprehended, he'd refused to reveal who had hired him. Imani had informed him that the Leonetti Vineyards property had been spared, along with their company and several smaller ranches. Although the Porters were into oil, and not ranching, Jonathan felt a modicum of empathy for the ranchers. People did not go into business with the purpose of becoming prey for thieves or saboteurs.

Emerald Ridge was an hour's drive east of Dallas, so Jonathan settled back on the leather seat, closed his eyes, and willed his mind blank to prepare for whatever he would be confronted with once he met with the attorney.

The driver maneuvered into the circular driveway leading to his house and Jonathan was fully alert when the vehicle came to a complete stop. After getting out, he walked to the front door of the sprawling Tuscan-style farmhouse he'd purchased six weeks after Danielle broke up with him. At that time, he'd grown tired of living in the two-bedroom rental townhome apartment in Chatelaine, where his neighbors monitored his comings and goings. And once he saw the house in Emerald Ridge, which was reminiscent of the ones he'd admired during his travels in Italy, he couldn't resist purchasing it. It contained six bedrooms and eight baths, and with more than six thousand square feet of living space set on five acres, Jonathan knew it was where he'd wanted to live. It was a big change from what he'd referred to as his bachelor pad, because he'd come to value his privacy.

Now, at thirty-two, Jonathan had stopped what he'd thought of as merry-go-round dating and become not only more selective, but also more discriminating when choosing to date. Living and traveling between the States and Dubai had changed him and his focus on growing Porter Oil was now a priority, while his love life was a distant second.

He lifted the cover on the door handle and punched in the code before opening the door. He entered in another combination on the wall panel next to the entrance to deactivate the security system. Cool air feathered over his face as he stepped into the foyer. The driver followed him into the house, handing him his carry-on. Jonathan took the bag at the same time he slipped a hundred-dollar bill into the man's hand.

"Thank you."

Jonathan smiled and nodded at the driver. "You're welcome."

The company had several drivers on call to accommodate his grandfather, Hammond Porter—Porter Oil's CEO—and other senior-ranking employees to take them to and from their destinations, while Jonathan preferred driving his Porsche Cayenne. Whenever he was in Dubai, Imani would occasionally take the SUV out to keep the engine running, and she had also assumed the responsibility of seeing that a cleaning service came to his home twice a month to clean and make certain everything was in working order.

Not only was he close to his sister, but they were also close in age, being only eleven months apart. His nephew, Colt Fortune Porter, was now seven months old, and if he had a son who was eleven months, then that would make them first cousins…

He shook his head as if to banish the possibility that he had fathered a child. It couldn't possibly be true, could it? Because if it were, his life would change irrevocably. Rather than mentally beat himself up, he adjusted the thermostat and made his way to the master bedroom and en suite bath to prepare for the inevitable.

A short time later, Jonathan ran a hand over his face, unable to believe what he had just read. There was DNA verification, a birth certificate, and photographs of a little baby boy who was without a doubt his Mini-Me.

He wasn't surprised Danielle Matthews had refused to tell him she was pregnant after he'd revealed he was flat broke. What she hadn't known at the time was that it was something he'd told those he dated to see if they would stick around, and that he was interested in women who wanted to be with him, not because he belonged to the wealthiest Black family in Texas. Danielle failed the test, and she had turned the tables on him by secretly having his child. A son she would have continued to withhold from him if she hadn't discovered she was terminally ill and wanted her son to know his father because she had grown up not knowing her own father. It had become the selfless act of a dying woman who had grown up in the foster care system and did not want the same for her son.

Danielle Matthews had given her son the masculine derivative of her first name, and her surname for the middle name, while listing Jonathan Porter as the child's father. The little boy he hadn't known existed until today was legally named Daniel Matthew Porter.

"Where is the boy now?" Jonathan asked the attorney, as he struggled inwardly not to exhibit the anxiety holding him captive. It was real. He was a father and he had to get his head and his life together before going into take charge CEO mode!

Warren Eliott rested his hand on a stack of file folders on the cherrywood conference table. "He's with a foster family. Once I call the social worker handling the case, she will arrange for the child to be picked up and delivered to me."

"How long will that take?"

"It can be done within forty-eight hours."

Jonathan closed his eyes and took deep breaths in an attempt to slow down his rapid breathing. Forty-eight hours ago he didn't know or could not have imagined that he would be a father. That was then and this was now, and he had to ready himself for the inevitable. He needed at least one day to purchase the things he needed to care for a baby—things he knew nothing about. And that meant he had to set up a room in house as a nursery. He'd thought about contacting his administrative assistant to help him on what he needed, then changed his mind. He opened his eyes and was finally able to experience a modicum of calmness.

"Call the social worker and let her know to deliver the baby here the day after tomorrow. I need to make some changes in my home before I can bring him home." He had suggested having the social worker bring the child to the office on Saturday, because it was a day when the office was closed, and he would be able to leave with the boy without alerting the staff that he was now a father. However, Jonathan knew that despite how many precautions he took, it would still become a source of office gossip once it became public knowledge.

Warren smiled. "Consider it done."

Jonathan shook hands with the attorney and left without stopping to speak to anyone. The corporate headquarters were in Chatelaine, but Porter Oil also had an outpost in the Emerald Ridge Boulevard office building. Most of the employees were used to seeing him in the office for several weeks, and on rare occasions more than a few months, and then not seeing him again for an extended period, whenever he departed for the Middle East. He'd overheard some calling him the Shadow. They never knew when he would be in the States, other than his grandfather, or his administrative assistant, who was as tight-lipped as a government covert agent.

Jonathan sat in his vehicle, staring out the windshield as he attempted to process all he'd experienced in the past hour. He'd read documents, including a DNA match, and sworn affidavits Danielle had drawn up before she'd succumbed to kidney cancer. She'd been diagnosed with gestational diabetes and preeclampsia during her first trimester, and she'd refused to terminate the pregnancy. After delivering her baby, one of her kidneys failed completely. She'd been placed on dialysis three times a week, and as her condition deteriorated, she'd drawn up a will giving Jonathan Porter sole custody of her son.

What Jonathan could not understand was why she hadn't contacted him. He exhaled an audible breath. No matter how things may have ended between them, there had been a time when he'd loved Danielle, and he would have made certain she would have been provided the best available medical care, and that she wouldn't have had to go through it alone. Even if Danielle hadn't been pregnant with his child, he would have helped her in any way he could. Out of all the women he'd dated, Jonathan had believed she was different—that she would be the one he could see himself eventually marrying and settling down with. He started up the SUV and headed for a baby store in the shopping mall he hoped stocked everything he would need to set up a nursery.

Jonathan forced himself to get into bed and get some sleep or fall on his face, before getting up to tackle the number of bags and boxes lined up against two walls in the bedroom across the hall from the master suite. He had decided to set up the nursery close to his bedroom, where he could get to the baby more quickly than if he had set it up one in another wing of the house. What he had to do was stop thinking of the boy as the baby. He was his son, yet knew that would take time getting used to referring to Daniel as his son.

He still found it hard to believe he had fathered a child when he'd been so careful about using protection. This is not to say he didn't want to become a father, but only when he'd felt he was ready to assume the responsibility of taking care of a family. Well, life had thrown him a curve; he had less than two days to get ready.

The sales associate at the big-box baby store had helped him select whatever he needed. The furniture he'd selected was in the warehouse and was scheduled to be delivered the following day. From having limited interaction with babies, he had become overwhelmed with the number of things needed to care for one. And was beyond appreciative to the woman for sharing her knowledge and expertise, not to mention patiently answering his never-ending questions.

But baby paraphernalia aside, he knew he was way out of his league.

He had only seen his nephew, Colt, a few times, and whenever he visited his sister, it had been the little guy's naptime. And when he'd attempted to wake him up, Imani had read him the riot act, because it had become her time to do things she couldn't do whenever Colt was awake. He'd apologized, telling her he knew nothing about babies or their routines.

He was beginning to think karma was repaying him for not being truthful in the past. But now that he was a father with an eleven-month-old, dating was out of the question anyway. Jonathan knew he had to tell his family about Daniel, then decided to wait until after he'd picked up the boy. He shook his head. It was no longer *the boy* or *the baby*, but his son.

When he entered the attorney's office Saturday morning to find the social worker holding Daniel, Jonathan experienced an emotion so foreign that he was at a loss for words. Daniel had been asleep, then suddenly awakened, as if to see who this big man was with a face that looked like his own.

Seeing his son in person was even more disturbing than staring at a photograph because the resemblance between the two of them was uncanny. In fact, if Jonathan's baby pictures were placed side by side with Daniel's, it would have been impossible to distinguish one from the other.

Jonathan sucked in a breath as if to garner the confidence needed to care for a baby who, for all intents and purposes, was a stranger. It wasn't as if he'd been with Danielle during her pregnancy or had witnessed the birth of their son, to prepare him for what it meant to be a father. Now, it was as if he'd been thrown into the deep end of the pool and was forced to learn to swim.

He'd had two days to prepare to take his son home, a home with a nursery outfitted with everything essential for the comfort and well-being of a baby. After he had recovered from the time change, he'd thrown all his energy into setting up the nursery. But it wasn't until the furniture had been delivered, and all the baby food he'd ordered online had arrived, that he was truly able to exhale.

The middle-age social worker smiled, introducing herself as Ms. Thomas, jarring him back to the present. "Would you like to hold your son, Mr. Porter?"

Jonathan took a tentative step forward and held out his arms, not knowing quite what to expect. But the instant he felt the warm body against his chest, he realized being a father filled him with a strange comfort, and all was right in his world. He met the large, round, dark brown eyes in a chubby face the color of toffee candy. Daniel was dressed in a blue-and-white striped seersucker romper, and light blue socks, and white soft-bottom shoes adorned his tiny feet.

"He's a lot heavier than he looks."

"That's because his foster mother claims he has a ro- bust appetite," Ms. Thomas said as she picked up a large, quilted tote bag. "His diapers and bottles are in here, while his clothes and a few books are in the carry-on. His foster mom also wrote out what he likes to eat, and the times for feedings and his nap."

Jonathan took a quick glance at the suitcase in a corner of the office, wondering how he was going to carry Dan- iel, the tote bag, and the carry-on to his car in the parking lot. He'd witnessed mothers with several children in tow attempting to keep them together while getting them into a vehicle with car seats. It was no doubt they would have had to develop a routine or were truly superwomen.

"Not to worry, Mr. Porter. I'll help you down to your car. Oh, I forgot to ask. Do you have a child's car seat?" the social worker asked.

"Yes."

"Good. Now, I need you to sign a release, then you can take your son home."

Holding Daniel with one arm, Jonathan scrawled his signature on several documents. Ms. Thomas put one in her handbag, gave another to Warren Eliott, and then the final one to Jonathan.

Now, he could take his son home.

Daniel had fallen asleep during the ride back to the house, and when Jonathan lifted him out of the car seat, he hadn't woken up. Which he had been eternally grateful for because, honestly, he didn't have a clue as to how to soothe a fussy or crying baby. He was still zonked out when Jonathan removed his shoes, socks, and romper. Clothed only in a disposal diaper and undershirt, Daniel was lying on his back in the crib, his little chest rising and falling as his tiny mouth made sucking sounds.

Jonathan had realized he had been holding his breath as he watched his son sleep. He suddenly recalled Imani telling him that she managed to get a lot of things done whenever Colt was asleep, so he decided it was time to set up the baby monitors. He positioned them in his bedroom and the kitchen, as well as the family room, then went through the contents of the tote bag and carry-on.

He put two six-ounce bottles of milk in the fridge. Jonathan smiled when he took out a glass container with Cheerios. There were notes outlining the foods Daniel preferred. The eleven-month-old was on solid food, but it had to be either finely chopped or puréed. He drank from a sippy cup but liked a bottle of milk before going to sleep at night. And he was sensitive to peaches, and loved bananas and pears.

Jonathan also found a binder with his medical information, including vaccinations. He made a mental note to ask Imani for the name of her pediatrician. There was obviously a lot more to taking care of a baby than he'd believed. Bath times, nap times, feedings, changing diapers, and so on.

Thankfully, the foster mother's notes were detailed. Going through them, he'd learned that Daniel was crawling and pulling up to stand, while he couldn't walk unaided. He was attempting to talk, and the only thing she'd understood was his occasionally saying *Da-da.* He was now sleeping throughout the night and only cried when he was hungry or needed to be changed. Jonathan decided to Face-Time his sister now that Daniel was napping. Going into the kitchen, he tapped Imani's number on his cell phone.

"Hey, bro. What's up?" she asked when her image appeared on his screen.

Imani asking him what's up would no doubt come as complete shock when he told her what he'd discovered only two days ago. "I'm back in the States, and I just found out the other day that I'm a father."

Imani's eyes grew large. "Say what?" She paused. "You're kidding me, aren't you?"

Jonathan told her about the telephone conversation with Warren that had him flying back to Texas. He almost laughed when Imani's jaw dropped at the same time she grabbed her forehead, as if what he was telling her was too impossible to believe.

"She never told you she was pregnant?" Imani queried.

"Nope."

"Why wouldn't she?"

Jonathan gritted his teeth. "That's something I don't want to talk about on the phone."

"It was that bad?"

His sister was asking a litany of questions he really did not feel like discussing. At least not now. "I'll tell you everything when you come to meet your nephew."

"Fine." She looked unhappy but didn't press him any further. "Where is my little nephew and who else is in the loop?"

"He's napping, and right now, only you and Warren know about him. But after I hang up, I'm going to call Mom to let her know she has another grandson. Then I'll tell Dad."

"You can't call Mom because she and her sisters are spending two weeks at a spa in Arizona with a focus on peace and enlightenment. They're due back next weekend."

He huffed out a breath. "Why did they go all the way to Arizona when they could have taken advantages of the spa services here at the Fortune's Gold Ranch?"

"I asked them the same question and they said being in the desert was their wish to get closer to nature. Mom told me not to call her unless there is an emergency. And while you finding out that you have a son is definitely a shock, it doesn't exactly constitute an emergency. What I do suggest is that you hire a good nanny."

"I don't want to relinquish the care of Daniel to anyone else right now, because I plan to take a couple of weeks off to be a full-time father."

Imani laughed. "Wow. I'm really impressed. I can't believe my jet-setting, workaholic brother is stepping away from Porter Oil."

"Only for a few weeks. And I don't have to tell you how important family is to us." For Jonathan, being a Porter was like being a member of a royal Black family. "I meant to ask, how's Colt and Nash?" His sister's relationship with Nash Fortune had resulted in them becoming parents to a baby boy; she'd moved in with Nash and now they were planning their future together as a family.

"They are both good. As soon as I get a break, I'll bring Colt over to introduce him to his cousin."

Jonathan ended the call when he heard Daniel's cries through the monitor. He was up from his nap. He changed him, fed him lunch, and then selected one of the books his foster mom had packed and read to him. To his relief, the baby was content to sit on his lap and appeared to be listening as he read a book with repetitive rhyming.

Once Daniel began wiggling, Jonathan put him on the floor, where he crawled to the glider's ottoman and pulled himself up to stand. Smiling down at his son, Jonathan applauded, and when the baby let go to clap his hands, too, he fell on his bottom. He appeared startled and crawled back to where Jonathan sat on the glider.

Leaning over, he scooped up Daniel and held him against his chest. "It's okay, little guy. How about I take you outside to show you where you will play once you're able to run around?" Dipping his head, he pressed a kiss on the soft curls. "And I'm willing to bet once you discover baseball, I will have to have a glazier on speed dial to replace broken windows." He grinned despite himself. "I can't tell you how many windows I broke before my father banned me from playing ball so close to the house. Fortunately, there's enough space on the property to put up a play area for you, and when you're older I'll put up a basketball hoop. I've already thought about installing an in-ground pool, too. But first, you will have to learn to swim." Daniel smiled and blathered about something. "Yes. It's just you and me, and that makes us Team Porter, and we don't need anyone else."

He continued his rambling while reclining on a hammock under the gazebo covering an outdoor kitchen. Daniel lay against his chest, clutching and sucking on the fabric of Jonathan's shirt. "I think a teething ring would do a lot better than my shirt." Then without warning, his son bit him, laughing hysterically once Jonathan let out a gasp. "So, you think that's funny, do ya?" Daniel laughed even harder, displaying a mouth with two top and two lower teeth, with another two in the bottom, peeking through the gums.

Boy, he sure was adorable.

Jonathan rolled off the hammock while cradling Daniel close to his body and returned to the house for a teething ring. Daniel hadn't bitten him hard enough to break the skin, but he didn't want his son to get into a habit of biting.

It was later, when they were lying together on a daybed in the nursery, with Daniel gnawing on the teething ring, that Jonathan felt a peace that had often eluded him. His birthright as a Porter afforded him privilege few would ever experience or enjoy. As such, it had been drilled into him that he had to uphold not only the family name, but also Porter Oil. However, in that moment, Jonathan would have traded all of it because of the little boy for whom he was now responsible. Although he'd had no experience with babies, in that instant, he vowed to be the best father he could be.

After giving Daniel his bath and putting him in his crib for the night, Jonathan felt as if he'd scaled a huge hurdle. He had survived day one as a daddy. All was quiet as he went into his home office to send his father an email, to tell Phillip that he was now a grandfather for the second time. He knew the news would be as shocking to his dad as it had been to him. After logging off and shutting down the computer, Jonathan left the office for the family room to watch a baseball game on TV. As an unabashed sports junkie, when living abroad it had been the sporting events that he missed most, other than his family.

After graduating college he'd become a jet-setter, visiting countries on his wish list until his father was able to secure oil leases in Dubai. Then he'd begun to divide his time between the States and the Middle East. Although the headquarters for Porter Oil was in Chatelaine, whenever he was in the country, Jonathan oversaw the outpost several miles outside of Emerald Ridge, where the company owned a few oil wells.

Once the Texas Rangers game ended, he turned off the television and made his way to the foyer to activate the alarm. As he did so, he recognized the sound of a car peeling out, so he ran to the door. He opened it and went outside just in time to see the taillights of a pickup speeding away.

Jonathan went completely still when he saw that a family heirloom garden sculpture was missing from the walkway.

He smothered a curse. It wasn't the only thing he noticed. He spotted a bandana on the ground where the thief had apparently dropped it. "Who the hell left this?" Leaning closer, Jonathan recognize the logo of the Fortune's Gold Ranch. Instinct told him not to the touch the bandana because if there was DNA, then maybe the police would be able to identify the thief.

Returning to the house, he picked up his phone and searched for the number to the ranch. The phone rang twice before a woman answered. "Fortune's Gold Ranch. This is Vivienne."

Jonathan cleared his throat. He'd heard Vivienne Fortune was the forewoman, and if they had acknowledged each other over the years, it was always in passing. "Ms. Fortune—"

"Please call me Vivienne, Jonathan," she said, interrupting. "What do I owe the pleasure of your call?"

You won't be so friendly after I tell you that one of your employees just stole a family heirloom from me.

Jonathan filled in Vivienne about the missing embellished Zen master meditating statue and that the thief had dropped a bandana with the ranch's logo.

Are you accusing someone from my ranch of being a thief?" she spat out angrily.

"If the shoe fits … then wear it," he retorted.

"What's that supposed to mean?"

"You need to see what I'm talking about. As soon as I hang up, I'm going to call the police."

She huffed out a breath. "Fine. I'll be right over."

Jonathan heard the tone indicating she had hung up. He made a second call. This time to the local police.

Chapter Two

He didn't have to wait long for Vivienne to arrive, and when she stepped out of the pickup, he was slightly taken aback by her appearance. Long, blond waves floated around her face, over her shoulders, and down her back; it was her hair that had immediately struck him, because whenever their paths had crossed, her hair was usually styled in a single braid or a ponytail. Over the years, his interactions with her had been limited to an occasional smile or nod. But that was then and this was now. And judging from her expression, which was illuminated by the solar lighting surrounding the property, Jonathan knew she was upset.

In fact, he swore he could feel the hostility radiating from Vivienne Fortune when she stopped less than a foot away from him. He wondered why she was so angry, when it was *he* who was the victim of a theft.

"Are you actually accusing someone from my ranch of being a thief?" she spat out angrily, repeating what she'd asked on the phone.

He pointed to the bandana on the ground. "I'm certain you are more than familiar with this. Or is this the first time you're seeing it?" he asked sarcastically.

"It does belong to FGR, but everyone has a few of them," she said, bending over to pick it up.

"Don't touch it!" Jonathan shouted, and Vivienne pulled back. "I've called the police, and they can use it as evidence that it could belong to someone connected with your ranch."

Vivienne's shoulders slumped and Jonathan realized some of the fight had gone out of her. "You're not the only one who has been victimized by a rash of thefts and sabotage. My ranch has been hit, too."

Jonathan nodded. "I've heard about the problems that have afflicted some of the ranchers. But that still wouldn't stop a disgruntled employee of perpetrating the thefts and sabotage to throw suspicion off them."

"That's preposterous! I trust all my employees. And in case you haven't heard, my brother, Micah, went undercover to identify the thief, who just happens to have a lengthy rap sheet. After his arrest, he pled guilty, yet he has refused to disclose who'd hired him."

"Where is he?"

"In the county jail awaiting sentencing."

Jonathan met her eyes. He wanted to tell Vivienne that she was being naive but held his tongue. If her brother caught one thief on their ranch, there still could be others. Arguing with her wasn't going to solve the problem that someone had criminally trespassed on his property and stolen an item that held warm memories for the Porters. That the person they had in custody could belong to a group of thieves preying not only on local ranchers, but also residents.

"Now, since we must wait for the police, why don't you come inside for coffee?" He'd offered Vivienne an olive branch. But it was only momentarily. However, there would be hell to pay if he found out that someone from her ranch had stolen the statue, because he wouldn't hesitate to press charges against the perpetrator.

"Okay," she said after a long pause. "By the way, how valuable is the statue?" she asked.

"Not only is it valuable. It's also a family treasure." He extended his arm toward the house. "Please, let's go in."

Vivienne could not—did not—want to believe that one of her employees was responsible for stealing a lawn statue from Jonathan Porter, because the man who had been apprehended and jailed had been charged with vandalism and theft at several ranches, not residential property. What had become so frustrating was the thief had refused to disclose who was behind the criminal ring targeting Emerald Ridge's most prosperous ranchers.

And despite her annoyance, she could not ignore that the man who had invited her into his home was the total package: tall, dark, gorgeous, and successful. Not only did he belong to the wealthiest Black family in Texas, but it was also rumored that the Porters might be as wealthy as the Fortunes. Which was saying something, given how big the Fortune family – and the scope of their businesses were.

Vivienne walked into the foyer and was stunned by the sheer vastness of Jonathan's mansion. Twin staircases, parquet floors in a herringbone design, an antique table positioned against a wall topped with artifacts from different countries and cultures, and light from an array of chandeliers that dotted the gleaming wood floors set the stage for luxurious living and entertainment.

She followed him through a great room and down a hall that opened out into an expansive kitchen that was a chef's dream, with top-of-the-line appliances, off-white walls, a colorful mosaic backsplash, royal blue cabinetry with brass knobs, and pale gray and darker blue quartz countertops. A copper range hood over the eight-burner stove matched the gleaming cookware suspended above the cooking island. It was obvious Jonathan had spared no expense when it came to decorating his home after he'd moved from Chatelaine to Emerald Ridge. Her eyebrows lifted slightly when she saw a high chair pulled up to a banquette in the kitchen's alcove. She assumed the chair was for his sister's son, Colt.

Vivienne's gaze drifted back to Jonathan as he washed his hands in one of the double stainless-steel sinks, then dried them on a towel. "How do you like your coffee?" he asked her.

"Oh, I get a choice?"

Jonathan glared at her. "You will for now. That is until I uncover who at your ranch stole my property.

Vivienne struggled not to lose her temper. Yes, she understood he was upset because someone had stolen his property and left what he considered evidence; however, she felt he was being premature when he'd accused someone from her ranch as the thief.

"There's no need to be testy with me, Jonathan. After all, I'm not your thief…or your enemy. Let me remind you that you're not the only one who has been targeted. Fences were sabotaged where cattle had escaped and also the theft of valuable horses and pricey saddles.

He went completely still. "Did I say you were a thief?"

"No. But you did insinuate that maybe one of my ranch hands may be.

"Don't try and put words in my mouth, Vivienne."

"Weren't you the one who'd mentioned a disgruntled employee?" She held up her hand when he opened his mouth. "I'm done talking about this. Let's wait until the police get here to see what they come up with." Vivienne pointed to the espresso machine on a countertop. "And I'll have a cappuccino, thank you."

* * *

Jonathan slowly blinked. He realized Vivienne had just dismissed him as if he was a child whose mother had given him a you-don't-want-to-mess-with-me look. There was something about her demeanor that indicated she could more than hold her own as the forewoman of a multithousand-acre ranch. And despite his suspicion that one of her employees could be responsible for stealing his lawn statue, he had to respect her because she was willing to defend them unconditionally.

Jonathan had also admired that although she belonged to a prominent ranching family, she hadn't morphed into the role of a rich girl flaunting her status with designer clothes, luxury cars, or precious jewelry. Instead, she had rolled up her sleeves and had gotten her hands dirty, learning to become a forewoman of a huge cattle ranch that included managing the staff. And if she didn't choose to work, then she could've spent her days at the guest ranch's spa. Even if she hadn't been born into wealth, her willingness to embrace hard work told Jonathan she never would have become like some of the gold diggers he'd dated in the past.

He was aware that it had taken a lot of blood, sweat and tears for her to become the forewoman of Fortune Gold's cattle operation. And it was common knowledge in Emerald Ridge that she'd finally won the trust of her father, Hayden Fortune, to rise to that position.

"One cappuccino coming up," he said under his breath. "Whole milk or nondairy creamer."

"Whole milk is okay."

Jonathan gathered the items he needed to make Vivienne's coffee. All the while, he felt, rather than saw, her blue eyes following his every motion as she sat on a stool at the breakfast island. Although annoyed that she was blatantly defensive when it came to the possibility that some-one from her ranch may have stolen the statue, Jonathan had to acknowledge that she was incredibly beautiful. He'd found her long palomino-gold hair and sparkling blue eyes mesmerizing. And he hadn't missed the feminine curves of her slim hips in a pair of fitted jeans. She was also tall, a lot taller than women he usually found himself attracted to, yet that hadn't stopped him from admiring her slender figure.

The distinctive aroma of brewing coffee filled the kitchen, a smell Jonathan believed was akin to ambrosia, and after he'd topped the steaming brew with a thick layer of steamed milk, he set the cup in front of Vivienne. "Enjoy."

She met his eyes. "Aren't you going to have one?" she asked when he turned off the machine.

Jonathan shook his head. "I'll have one later..." His words trailed off when the sound of a baby crying came through the monitor on the banquette table. "Excuse me." Turning on his heels, he raced out of the kitchen and up the staircase to the nursery. Daniel was standing up and crying as he supported himself while holding on to the side of the crib. Reaching over, he picked up the baby, cradling him to his chest. "It's okay. Daddy's going to take care of his big boy." He recalled the foster mother's note that Daniel cried at night when he was hungry or needed changing. It took him less than three minutes to remove a wet diaper and replace it with a new one. He was finally getting the hang of removing the wet diaper and replacing it with a clean one before getting sprayed, because the first time he'd made the attempt he'd been forced to change both Daniel and himself.

When Jonathan returned to the kitchen carrying Daniel, Vivienne nearly choked as she swallowed a mouthful of coffee and she stared at him over the rim of her cup.

"I had no idea that you had a child," Vivienne said, once she recovered from her obvious shock.

"Neither did I until a couple of days ago—"

Jonathan's explanation stopped abruptly because he didn't want to reveal too much to someone who wasn't family. Daniel's existence wasn't any of Vivienne's business and if he revealed the circumstances behind his son's existence, it wouldn't make him look good.

Slipping off the stool, Vivienne smiled at the baby, who spit out the pacifier that was attached to a colorful ribbon on his onesie and gave her what passed for a smile, revealing tiny white teeth resembling grains of rice.

"He is so adorable." She met Jonathan's dark eyes, which seemed to penetrate straight through her. "What's his name and how old is he?" she asked.

"Daniel is eleven months."

"He's older than Colt."

Since she and Nash Fortune were related, Vivienne was aware that he and Jonathan's sister had had a brief three-month liaison. She didn't know the full story, but there was gossip that Imani broke up with him when Nash said he didn't want children. It was only after the breakup that Imani had discovered she was pregnant. Imani subsequently had become involved with a man willing to marry her and become a father to the child she was carrying. Eight months pregnant, wearing wedding attire, and standing before a justice of the peace at a town hall in Stone Crest, Texas, about to marry a man she did not love, Imani had become a runaway bride. Rumor was she had been harboring doubts that her fiancé's reason for proposing marriage was strictly financial. After all, it was a well-known fact that Imani Porter was in line to inherit her grandfather's ranch in Cactus Grove, which had a very lucrative oil field.

When Vivienne heard the news about Imani and her cousin's subsequent reunion, to her it was straight off the pages of a romance novel when Imani fled the town hall and went into labor. She'd parked on the side of the road, and the man who rescued her and delivered her baby was none other than Nash Fortune, who'd had no idea that he'd delivered his son.

Vivienne wondered about Jonathan and his baby mama, because although she would occasionally see him around town whenever he was in the country, she could not remember ever seeing him with a woman after he'd moved to Emerald Ridge. Even when he'd lived in Chatelaine his dating exploits had not become fodder for those seeking to label Jonathan Porter as an eligible-bachelor playboy.

But if he had, in fact, gotten married, then where was his wife? And if not, then who and where was Daniel's mother? But she wasn't about to ask Jonathan, who was shooting her with what she interpreted as his death stare. The impasse ended with the chiming of the doorbell, and what she assumed were the police.

She'd finished drinking the excellently prepared cappuccino when Jonathan ushered two young officers into the kitchen, and he explained to them what had happened. Vivienne listened to the police officers asking Jonathan the same questions they'd asked her and the other ranchers about the thefts, as if they were reading from a script they had rehearsed over and over. They weren't certain whether the theft of the missing statue was related to the others thefts, but because the FGR bandana was left at the scene, it could mean one of her ranch hands could also be on the mastermind's payroll.

Or it might just be an isolated incident.

Jonathan had suspected that someone at her ranch could possibly be involved with the thefts and sabotage, and now the police were suggesting the same. Vivienne still didn't want to believe the presumed allegations, but there was one way to find out, and that was to address it directly with her ranch hands.

As one officer droned on about the items stolen from various ranches, items Vivienne was more than aware of, she found herself studying the incredibly handsome man who was tenderly and protectively cradling his son. She smiled when the baby sighed audibly, closed his eyes, and drifted back off to sleep with the pacifier in his mouth.

She sighed. Gosh, what a precious sight… Suddenly, something garnered Vivienne's attention again. One of the officers was talking about the man who had been apprehended on the Fortune's Gold Ranch. He was saying the perp could possibly be involved with a band of thieves targeting wealthy ranches. Her pulse raced. This was the first time she'd heard that law enforcement suspected there might be more than one individual connected to the crimes. Was it possible that the police were now on to something? And with the alleged perpetrator behind bars, there was no way he could have stolen Jonathan's lawn statue. There had to be another thief—or thieves—out there and that gave her pause when she recalled Jonathan mentioning a disgruntled employee attempting to divert suspicion elsewhere. While she still couldn't wrap her mind around someone working for FGR being responsible for the crimes, there *was* the bandana left on the ground near where the missing statue had been. Evidence that may prove that one of her ranch hands could be on the mastermind's payroll. But the Fortune's Gold Ranch employees were well paid, and were offered health insurance, paid vacation, and bonuses. Why, she thought, would any of them risk being arrested or imprisoned?

Suddenly, she prayed this was an isolated incident after all.

A police officer gave Jonathan his card, telling him they would follow up by examining the bandana for forensic evidence, and would keep him abreast of any news about the theft of the missing ten-pound marble lawn statue.

Vivienne followed Jonathan as he escorted the deputies through the house and outside, then watched as they drove away. She met his eyes as the light from gaslight lanterns flanking the front door bathed him in a flattering golden glow that made it impossible for her to look away. It was as if she'd been swept up in a force field from which there was no escape. The soporific spell was shattered by the sound of Daniel's soft grunting before he settled back to sleep in his daddy's arms.

"I'm going to talk to my ranch hands tomorrow and let you know what I find out. And as for the bandana, anyone could have gotten ahold of it because we give them away at local and promotional events."

Jonathan narrowed his eyes at her. "If you say so."

"I *do* say so, Jonathan." Vivienne did not want to believe that he was like a dog with a bone, refusing to let go of his suspicion that one of her people was responsible for the theft of his lawn statue.

A beat passed, then he nodded. "You have my number, so please call and let me know what you've come up with."

Vivienne smiled. There was a note of warmth in his voice that hadn't been there earlier. "Oh, I forgot to ask. I

know you said you were going to give the police a photo
of the statue, but could I also have one so I could photo-
copy it and hand out to the crew in case someone spots it?"

Jonathan nodded again. "Okay. You can come over and
pick it up wherever you have time."

"What about tomorrow around noon?"

"Noon is fine. Although I've filed a police report, I'm
going to hold off contacting the insurance company about
the theft because hopefully the police will be able to make
an arrest."

Vivienne was hoping the same. "I'll see you tomorrow
then. Good night, and good luck with Daniel."

"Thank you, and you have a good evening as well."
There was just a hint of a smile lifting the corners of his
mouth.

She made her way to where she'd parked her vehicle, got
in, and maneuvered out of the driveway. As she headed in
the direction of the ranch, her head spun with everything
that had transpired since she'd picked up her phone to answer Jonathan Porter's call.

Coming to his home was her first personal interaction
with the wealthy young oilman. Seeing him up close and
talking to him, along with the knowledge that he had fathered a son, had left Vivienne feeling slightly off balance.
However, that paled in comparison when she thought about
who could have had it in for him that they would trespass
on his property to steal something that was prized by the
Porters. Knowing the thieves might not just be targeting
ranchers left Vivienne feeling even more uneasy about the
crimes. Now, someone was potentially threatening private
residences, too.

Damaging property was one thing, but she didn't want
to think of it escalating to personal injury. The Porters

were affluent, and it appeared as if the thief or band of thieves could be harboring a grudge against those who had accumulated wealth. She exhaled a shaky breath. The sooner the ringleader was identified, the better, before something worse than property loss—like loss of human life—occurred.

She shook her head as if she could banish all thoughts about the thefts. Jonathan's phone call had interrupted what Vivienne planned for a night of self-care. She'd wanted to take a leisurely bubble bath, then get into bed and watch a couple of episodes of a favorite period drama that was in its third season. It wasn't often that she was able to indulge in watching what she'd deemed a guilty pleasure, where she found herself transported back in time when a young woman's sole focus was falling in love and finding her happily ever after.

Vivienne didn't mind living vicariously through the fictional heroines because her own love life was practically nonexistent. It wasn't that she couldn't attract men. They were all just so wrong for her. Whenever they heard the name *Fortune*, it was as if their eyes would light up with dollar signs. One had even called her his *sugar mama*, which had disappointed her because she'd become quite fond of him. Once the evening ended, she sent him a text telling him it was over, and if he attempted to step a foot on the FGR ranch, he would be arrested for trespassing. Then she blocked his number.

It had been more than a year since her last date, and as the forewoman for the cattle ranch, she'd had little time to develop meaningful relationships. It had taken years as her father's apprentice to acquire the knowledge for the position, but it was her flexibility that had won over his approval. In the end, Hayden Fortune had to admit his daughter was qualified for the position, and over time, the ranch hands had come to accept and respect her.

Her workday didn't start at nine and end at five, but began at sunrise and occasionally went beyond sunset. Her responsibilities for overseeing a three-thousand-acre cattle ranch included interviewing and hiring ranch staff, and making promotion recommendations to her brother Micah, FGR's CEO. She also had to ensure that daily and weekly chores were completed, as well as direct and oversee the maintenance and repair of buildings, houses, vehicles, and ranch equipment.

After parking the pickup at the rear of her house, Vivienne entered through the back door. The cabin was one of six on the ranch built a little more than a quarter mile apart to allow for maximum privacy for each. Her parents, Hayden and Darla Fortune, shared the main ranch house with Hayden's cousin Garth Fortune and Garth's wife, Shelley. Vivienne and her brothers grew up in the right wing of the mansion, while her cousins grew up in the left wing. All the cousins were able to move out of the mansion and into their own homes on the property, as gifts from their parents once they'd turned twenty-one.

Vivienne left her boots in the mudroom and walked on sock-covered feet to her bedroom, her mind swirling with what she needed to tell her brothers about yet another theft and the possibility that someone at their ranch could be the perpetrator.

Just because she had a miserable ending to her day, she decided to wait until the following morning to call Micah and Drake because she didn't want to ruin their night. Besides, nothing could be done at this hour with many of the ranch hands settling in for the night. Vivienne still planned to take a bubble bath, but catching up on the episodes of her favorite period series would have to wait for another time.

She walked into the en suite bathroom, then turned on the water in the soaking tub, added a capful of lavender bath salts, and lit several candles that lined a marble-topped table. She smiled as the aroma of her favorite flowers filled the expansive space. Vivienne loved the bathroom in the master suite, decorated in hues of monochromatic blues and green. Wall sconces resembling Victorian gaslights, hand-painted glazed pots overflowing with live plants, and re-laxing music that flowed through concealed speakers had turned her bathroom into a private spa. Although there was the Fortune's Gold Ranch Guest Ranch Spa, Vivienne usu-ally availed herself of their services for massages, mani-pedis, and facials. However, she was past due on those treatments because she'd been much too occupied with hav-ing to deal with the sabotage.

After stripping off her clothes and leaving them in a hamper, she pulled her hair into a topknot and then slipped into the warm bubbly water, sighing audibly as she rested her head against the rim of the tub. Closing her eyes, she thought about her interaction with Jonathan Porter. Not only was it the first time that she had been in his home, but she'd also been close enough to discern things about him to which she hadn't been aware. In the past and whenever their paths had crossed, she'd thought of him as the con-summate wealthy oilman wearing tailored Western-styled business suits, boots, and a Stetson. Then there was daddy Jonathan in jeans, a white T-shirt that displayed a pair of broad shoulders, and with muscled biceps, who'd gently cradled his son against his solid chest.

Vivienne smiled as she sank lower in the tub. There was no doubt about it—Daniel's father was tall, dark, and gorgeous. Just as quickly, however, her smile faded, as she recalled Jonathan's accusation that maybe one of her ranch hands could be responsible for stealing his statue. She'd wanted to tell him, *"Cool your jets, hotshot, because you could get in more trouble than you could get out of making baseless accusations."*

Even when she had reminded him that her ranch hadn't been exempt from the vandalism, she suspected he still didn't believe her. What Jonathan hadn't known was all FGR employees were vetted before they were approved for hire. However, she wasn't about to try and convince the man that her people weren't thieves, but she would do whatever she could to uncover the mastermind.

Twenty minutes later, the bubbles were fading, the water had cooled, and Vivienne knew it was time to get out of the tub. She went through a ritual of patting the moisture from her body with a thick velour towel before slathering on moisturizer, a sample she had picked up from the FGR spa. She was pleased that Annelise Wellington's skin-care line, AW GlowCare, was as good as it had been advertised and was selling well at the spa.

She opened an armoire and took out a cotton nightgown, slipped it on, then extinguished the candles before walking into her bedroom. Vivienne got into bed, but discovered she was too wound up to go to sleep. The telephone call from Jonathan Porter, and the revelation that he had become the latest Emerald Ridge victim of a theft, had unnerved her. How many more, she wondered, would there be before all the thieves were apprehended?

She picked up the book off the bedside table and opened it. Although she'd downloaded several electronic books to her tablet, Vivienne still preferred reading a physical book.

She'd found turning the pages more rewarding than swiping across a screen.

Her mother had teased her, saying she was a nineteen-century woman in a twenty-first-century woman's body, because of her fascination with women who'd lived during the Regency, Victorian, and Gilded Ages. And when Darla Fortune had questioned her daughter about this, Vivienne told her mother that women during that time were less conflicted when it came to love and marriage. They'd hoped to marry for love, and if they hadn't been in love with their husbands because of an arranged marriage, then with time there was the possibility they would come to love them. And although it was frowned upon during those periods, women who chose to remain single would be able to live their lives by their leave, like she was doing.

What her mother didn't know was that Vivienne had all but given up on love and marriage. It wasn't that she was opposed to it, but that she had struck out so many times when it came to forming a relationship, and she was so focused as FGR's forewoman, that she had little or no time to date anyone. She managed to read several chapters in the book before her eyes started to close, and Vivienne knew it was time to go to sleep. She set the alarm on her cell phone, turned off the bedside lamp, and fell asleep within minutes of her head touching the pillow.

"Do you have any idea of what time it is?"

"I know exactly what time it is, Micah," Vivienne said to her brother. "But I need to run something by you. And I apologize if I interrupted something." She'd hoped her brother and sister-in-law weren't engaging in early morning lovemaking.

"Can't it wait until tomorrow?"

"No, it can't, Micah. Hold on, because I want to patch Drake in on our conversation." Her younger brother was less gruff when he answered the phone. It took Vivienne less than two minutes to tell them about her interaction with Jonathan Porter and that he and the police had mentioned the possibility that one or more of FGR's employees could be on the mastermind's payroll because the thief had dropped the ranch's bandana.

"I don't believe it!" Micah bit out. "Don't forget that I gave a basketful of FGR bandanas to a local promoter of a rodeo as giveaways a few months back. So, the thief could be anyone."

"Yeah, our people would never stoop to do something as low as that," Drake said.

"You're both singing to the choir," Vivienne countered. "I'm telling you this because I intend to call a meeting of the ranch hands, but only after I get a picture of the lawn statue from Jonathan. I'll hand out copies, and if someone from our ranch is culpable, then they will have to try and get rid of it. A ten-pound statue isn't something that can be easily hidden."

"Do you really believe our ranch hands are responsible for the thefts and sabotage?" Drake asked.

"No, but I need to make certain none of them are suspects if the police decide to come around asking questions," Vivienne replied.

"She's right, Drake," Micah said in agreement. "We need to squash this before it blows up into something more. I'm beginning to believe the person behind all that's been going on is a competitor who has decided to shift the focus from ranches to residences."

Vivienne nodded, although her brothers couldn't see her. "The only thing I'm going to say is Jonathan was not happy to find his family heirloom missing and our bandana left behind."

"Maybe I'll talk to him—"

"No, Drake," Vivienne said, cutting off her brother. "I'm the one who has been dealing with Jonathan."

"She's right," Micah repeated. "Let her handle this. She's the one Jonathan called, and he's agreed to give her a picture of the statue. What I'd like for you to do is be with her when she hands out copies of the photo of the statue during her morning meeting and watch for the reaction from each of the ranch hands. A guilty man will usually tip his hand."

Vivienne smiled, glad that she and Micah were on the same page here. Before calling her brothers, she'd scheduled early morning meetings to apprise everyone of what tasks she wanted the ranch hands to perform, and if one of them had stolen the statue, then it would be incumbent on him to get rid of the evidence quickly.

"I forgive you, Vivienne."

She quirked an eyebrow. "For what, Micah?"

"For calling me so early. You did good, kid."

"Ditto," Drake drawled. "I'm glad you were able to defuse the situation with Jonathan before we end up with another family feud on our hands."

"I might have been able to defuse it, but only temporarily," Vivienne warned.

The Fortunes feud with the Wellingtons had begun a century ago when a Fortune groom left a Wellington bride at the altar, totally humiliating her. Then a supposedly "skunked" bottle of thousand-dollar Leonetti wine was presented to the Wellingtons as an apology, escalating the bad blood between the families. No one knew how the wine had gotten ruined; however, it now brought the

Leonettis into the fray because they were furious that their impeccable reputation had been sullied.

It had taken decades, but the Fortunes managed to resume an amicable relationship with the Leonettis by exclusively offering their wines at the Fortune's Gold Guest Ranch and Spa. And now that Leo Leonetti and her cousin, Poppy Fortune, were planning to marry, Vivienne realized it would finally cement the two families.

She wasn't as certain with the Wellingtons because they'd always viewed the Fortunes as their competitors, while continuing to harbor the humiliation of a Wellington bride being jilted at the altar by a Fortune groom so many years ago. Vivienne did not want to think about the Wellington offspring because they'd had their own problems with their supposedly "evil stepmother," Courtney Wellington.

What she needed to focus on was the bandana left on Jonathan's property. Even though they were given away at several local events, the thief could have deliberately dropped it to shift the focus to her family's ranch. Who, Vivienne wondered, hated the Fortunes so much they would set her family up as the perpetrators?

Micah may have been instrumental in identifying one thief, and if there were more, then Vivienne vowed not to stop until all were arrested and charged.

Chapter Three

What Vivienne hadn't been able to see the night before as she drove along the paved road on Jonathan's property was the awe-inspiring sprawling mansion. It was as if someone had picked up the stone structure off a Tuscany countryside and set it down on a verdant plot of land in Emerald Ridge, Texas. There was something about his home that reminded her of the Leonetti Vineyards, combined with a gorgeous old Tuscan villa. She didn't know why, but somehow Vivienne had expected Jonathan's home to reflect his image as the quintessential wealthy oilman, with a ranch-style home, not this two-story Italian villa. But once again, she had to remind herself that she knew nothing about him other than he belonged to the wealthiest Black family in the state.

Then there was his son. If he had been married or involved with a woman, it had to have been a closely guarded Porter-family secret. Smiling, she thought about Daniel Porter. The little boy, who appeared to be his father's clone, was adorable. And watching Jonathan as he gently cradled his son to his chest had triggered a maternal instinct in Vivienne that up until now was totally foreign to her. Like most girls, she'd grown up believing she would fall in love and marry, but she hadn't gone as far to think about babies. It was as if having children for her was an afterthought, because becoming forewoman for the ranch had become so all-consuming that she had refused to think of anything else.

Her father had approved her to be the ranch's forewoman the year she'd turned twenty-seven, and now, at thirty-two, she had achieved everything she'd wanted and asked for. Professionally at least. Vivienne knew her mother was concerned that her only daughter would spend her life alone—that Darla would have to rely on her sons to give her grandchildren. Vivienne had reminded her mother countless times that she refused to be pressured into having a baby, and now that Micah was happily married to Jacinta Gomez, she should focus on them making her a grandmother.

Vivienne drove up alongside the house and came to a complete stop at the same time the front door opened, and Jonathan appeared holding Daniel. She got out and saw that the tall, handsome man was smiling, which was a good sign. Hopefully, she would not have to encounter any of last night's hostility, when she'd had to remind Jonathan that she wasn't his enemy. That the Fortunes were also victims.

"Good afternoon."

Jonathan nodded, his smile still in place. "Good afternoon to you, too. Daniel just finished eating lunch, so as soon as I put him down, we'll talk."

Vivienne shifted her gaze from father to son so Jonathan wouldn't see how much he was beginning to affect her. That just meeting his eyes made her pulse race, while at the same time heat spiraled through her body, silently reminding her of how long it had been since she'd shared a bed with a man.

What the heck is wrong with me? She didn't…no, she couldn't believe that she was lusting after a man who, despite fathering a child, she didn't know his status.

Was he married?

Divorced?

Widowed?

Or did he have a girlfriend, or even a fiancée?

Perhaps the reason for her dating drought was because she had been around too many men who she would never consider courting because they were her employees. And Vivienne had had a hard-and-fast rule never to mix business with pleasure, no matter how attractive she'd found the man.

Vivienne wanted to ask Jonathan what there was to talk about. She'd come for a photo of the statue, and then had planned to leave. Obviously, he had something else in mind. "All right." Daniel, wearing only an undershirt and diaper, was barefoot. He extended his arms to her. She met Jonathan's eyes. "Is it okay if I hold him?"

Jonathan laughed softly. "Yes."

She took the child, holding him to her chest. He felt warm and smelled wonderful. Lowering her chin, Vivienne pressed a light kiss to his dark, soft curls. Then, she rocked him gently and sang her favorite song, "You are my sunshine." By the time she'd finished the first verse, Daniel was laughing and babbling excitedly.

Jonathan stared at Vivienne, unable to believe his son was more animated than he had seen him since bringing him home. His foster mother had been right when she wrote Daniel only cried when he wanted to eat or needed to be changed. While Daniel was gabbing, most times Jonathan could not make out what he'd been saying. However, he did encounter a problem with him the day before when he'd put Daniel in his crib for his afternoon naptime; the baby would toss and turn, and occasionally cry because he didn't want to go to sleep. However, it was different last night, because after a warm bath and a bottle he would sleep throughout the night.

"Please, come in. Daniel needs to take his nap."

"He doesn't appear to be sleepy."

Jonathan met Vivienne's eyes. "Sleepy or not, I like to keep him to the schedule set up by his..." His words trailed off before he could say *foster mother*. He wasn't about to talk about Daniel's existence to anyone who wasn't family. As it was, he wasn't proud of the lies he'd told Danielle, resulting in her withholding the truth about her carrying his child. And he knew that was something he would have to disclose to his son when he was old enough to ask about his mother. And what he did not intend to do was lie to Daniel and thereby perpetuate another generation of lies. As it was, the Porters had their share of skeletons in the closet they preferred to keep hidden, because there were rumors about them not living up to their responsibilities.

"By whom?" Vivienne asked.

"It's not important," he countered. Jonathan waited for her to walk into the house, then closed the door to keep out the heat. It was early June and the high double digits made remaining outdoors during midday for any amount of time nearly impossible. He'd awoken that morning, brewed a cup of coffee, and sat on the loggia drinking it while watching the sun come up until the smoldering temperature forced him inside. He'd fared better with the desert heat because of the absence of the humidity, but it was entirely different in Texas.

While enjoying his morning brew, he'd thought about the curveball life had thrown him when he'd unexpectedly become a father. He hadn't realized until now that he was more a traditionalist than he'd known. He, like his parents, had wanted to fall in love, marry, and then start a family to add to another generation of Porters. That was then, and this was now. Daniel was his son, and it was his responsibility to not only take care of him, but also plan for his future.

Jonathan had sent Warren Eliott an email that he wanted to set up a meeting to draw up a will to provide for Daniel in the event something might happen to him. And if he decided to include a guardianship clause, then he would ask his sister, Imani, to become his son's legal guardian.

He led the way up a flight of stairs to the second story and down the hallway to the nursery. When the salesperson at the baby store had asked about the structural configuration in his home, Jonathan had mentioned that it wasn't on a single level, so she had recommended he purchase adjustable gates for the top and bottom of the staircases. Although Daniel wasn't walking yet, Jonathan had made it a practice to keep the top gate on both staircases secured.

Glancing over his shoulder at Vivienne, he noticed that Daniel had fallen asleep. "You must have the magic touch, because he doesn't like taking his afternoon nap."

She continued to hum softly as she gently rocked Daniel. "That's because you must sing to him."

"I don't sing. At least not nursery rhymes or baby songs. Come, and I'll show you where you can put him in his crib."

Vivienne entered the space Jonathan had set up as a nursery, finding it as sterile as a hospital's operating room. There was the off-white baby furniture, but other than that it lacked color. Where, she wondered, were the stuffed toys or colorful prints on the walls? Even a colorful area rug would make the room more inviting.

She placed Daniel on his back, watching the rise and fall of his little chest as he slept. She felt movement, then realized Jonathan was standing behind her. Close enough for her to feel warm breath feathering along the column of her neck. Desire thrummed through her like hot molten lava, and in that instant, she wanted to run out of his house to escape the traitorous feelings holding her captive. Why was her reaction to Jonathan Porter so different from what she'd experienced with other men? If she was honest with herself, he was a stranger to her; someone with whom she'd had little or no interaction other than acknowledging each other with a barely perceptible nod. Their paths had never crossed during local social events, and with him dividing his travels between the States and the Middle East, she could not recall the last time she'd seen him in person during those times.

Now, within the span of less than twenty-four hours of their interacting with each other, Vivienne did not know whether she was coming or going because her emotions were all over the place. It was as if Mother Nature had gone wild inside her, with a tsunami of desire that threatened to upend her life. She had to get what she'd come to Jonathan's house for and leave.

Quickly.

"I need you to get the photo because I'm expected back at the ranch to meet with someone." Heat flooded her face with the lie, but it was something she'd had to do.

Jonathan nodded. "Come with me."

They retraced their steps, Vivienne staring at Jonathan's broad shoulders under a white golf shirt, and the way his jeans hugged his slim hips and muscular thighs. It was obvious from his toned body that he hadn't spent all his time sitting behind a desk.

She followed him down the staircase and into a room on the first floor that he'd set up as a home office. Several desktop computers and a printer were lined up on a L-shaped workstation. Mahogany file cabinets, a small round conference table with four pull-up, dark blue leather chairs, and a wall of built-in bookcases set the stage for Jonathan to conduct Porter Oil business, whether in Texas or overseas.

Vivienne could not pull her gaze away from a corner table with a chessboard covered with jade-green chess pieces. And she'd noticed there were more figurines and objets d'art in jade, coral, and turquoise on the shelves of one of the bookcases. It was also packed tightly with books with subjects ranging from cooking, travel, mythology, art history, and archelogy. And what appeared to be a samurai sword rested on a stand that occupied its own shelf and captured her rapt attention. There was no doubt that Jonathan's interests were quite varied.

"This place is like a museum," she said, unable to conceal the awe in her voice.

"Everything here has been authenticated, appraised, and insured," Jonathan said when he saw her staring at the sword. "That's a replica, but when I saw it, I couldn't resist adding it to my collection."

She turned to face him. "Does *everything* include your lawn statue?"

He nodded. "Yes. I thought once I bought this house that I wouldn't have to install a gate to keep thieves out, but apparently, I was wrong."

A cold chill replaced the warmth Vivienne had experienced before. Jonathan's tone indicated he still believed someone at her ranch was responsible for stealing his family's heirloom. "Are you going to put up one now?"

"I'm seriously thinking about it. But what I'm planning to do is have the security company install cameras. That way I'll have a recording if someone decides to make another unannounced visit to steal something else."

"That's a good idea because now that you have Daniel, you need to keep him safe."

Vivienne mentioning keeping Daniel safe was like an alarm bell going off in Jonathan's head. It hadn't occurred to him that his son could become a kidnapping victim because, after all, he was a Porter. Installing gates with a security access code was more imperative than he'd originally thought.

And he hadn't been that removed from Emerald Ridge, because Imani was constantly updating him about events that had occurred whenever he was overseas working with his father. Everyone was gossiping about the baby abandoned on the Fortune's Gold Ranch doorstep with a note that the little boy was a Fortune. Then the rumor mill went into overdrive once there was an anonymous text that Baby Joey was Garth Fortune's son. The straw that broke the proverbial camel's back was when a woman claiming to be the child's mother said the Fortunes could keep the child, but she'd demanded a half million dollars for her pain and suffering in exchange for giving up her son.

An abandoned baby, extortion, multiranch sabotage, and *now* illegal trespassing and the theft of his family's heirloom lawn statue? Jonathan wondered what the hell he had come home to. There was enough drama in Emerald Ridge for a reality show.

"You're right, Vivienne. I need to do everything I can to protect my son."

"What about his mother?"

Jonathan went completely still. Several seconds passed before he was able to respond to Vivienne's query. And by the way she was looking at him, he knew she wanted an answer. "She's dead." The two words came out with the impact of dropping a large boulder from a high-rise, the rock falling and crashing onto the ground below, shattering into pieces when Vivienne put her hand over her mouth as if to retract the question. He noticed her eyes filling with tears.

"I'm sorry, Vivienne. I didn't mean it to come out like that."

Her eyelids fluttered when she lowered her hands and nodded. "I'm so, so sorry, Jonathan."

He took a step and rested his hand on her shoulder. He hadn't meant to upset her, but she'd asked, and he'd told her the truth. "It's okay. I've come to terms with it."

What he'd wanted to say was that it wasn't days ago, but a little more than a year ago that he'd come to the realization that what he'd had with Danielle Matthews was over. That despite his telling her he was broke, if she had continued to see him, then there was no doubt he would've proposed marriage. He'd administered the test, and she had failed miserably, because for her it was never about him, but Porter Oil.

The moisture filling Vivienne's eyes had turned them into pools of shimmering sapphires and Jonathan resisted the urge to kiss her and let her know that he and Daniel were okay. That there was no need for her to pity his situation. Dropping his hand, he turned and picked up a large envelope off the corner of the desk. "I can make copies if you want."

Vivienne shook her head. "That's not necessary. I'll make copies and then bring this back to you."

"You know where to find me."

She smiled. "That I do."

"I'll walk you out." It wasn't until he'd opened the passenger door of her pickup truck that he said, "Thank you for getting Daniel to settle down where he didn't put of a fight. He doesn't like napping."

Vivienne smiled. "There's no need to thank me. I happen to like kids." She paused. "By the way, your son's nursery needs a makeover."

His eyebrows shot up. "What are you talking about?"

"Other than the crib, no one would believe it's a place where a baby sleeps."

"What's wrong with it?"

"It needs color, Jonathan. Babies need stimulation. They need to see prints on the walls, with letters and numbers, and play with blocks and stuffed toys."

He folded his arms over his chest. "Do you have kids?"

"No, but I'm familiar with what is conducive to a child's stimuli because there is the Fortune's Gold Ranch day-care center."

He shot her a sheepish grin. "I suppose that would make you somewhat of an expert. I'm going to leave it up to you to buy what you need to make Daniel's nursery a show-place, and, of course, I'll reimburse you." He blew out a breath. "And I also want to apologize for jumping to con-clusions and accusing one of your people as the thief. I should've waited until the police came up with something more conclusive."

"Apology accepted. After I talk to my ranch hands and distribute pictures of your statue, maybe if we're lucky someone will come forward with the truth. Now, I'd like to make a request."

"And that is?" Jonathan asked, quirking an eyebrow.

"When I come back, I'd like another a cappuccino."

He winked. "Your wish is my command."

He waited for Vivienne to get in the pickup and stepped back when she started the engine. Even after the taillights had disappeared, Jonathan wasn't certain what to make of Vivienne Fortune. But if he had a checklist of five things that attracted him to a woman, there was no doubt she would come out a winner. She wasn't a gold digger, because she had been born into wealth. She was confident, otherwise she never would've passed the test to become forewoman of a three-thousand-acre cattle ranch. Vivienne was also feisty because nothing annoyed him more than a passive woman who did not stand up for herself. And, of course, she was beautiful, but honestly that didn't rank as high on his list as her other attributes. Then there was Daniel. It was apparent his son felt comfortable with her when he'd wanted her to hold him. Holding and singing to him had calmed the baby, and he'd fallen asleep in her arms.

Jonathan knew he couldn't afford to even begin to think about looking for a mother for his son, when he was just learning how to be a father. And if he did meet a woman, then she had to be willing to accept not only him, but also Daniel. After all, they were a package deal.

And there were times since bringing Daniel home that he'd thought about the baby's mother, recalling that Danielle Matthews was different from the other women with whom he'd been involved, and because she was, he'd found her intriguing. The first time he'd noticed her was when she was waitressing in a restaurant where he'd occasionally have lunch or dinner meetings. She was all business when taking orders and she never appeared flustered whenever male customers attempted to come on to her.

Her unflappable demeanor was tested when one customer who'd had too much drink touched her inappropriately and she dumped a glass of water in his lap. She'd tried explaining to the maître d' what had occurred, and she'd risked being fired on the spot if Jonathan hadn't intervened to tell what he'd witnessed, thereby saving her job.

Several weeks later, he'd returned to the restaurant and asked to be seated in her section. Danielle remembered him and thanked him for coming to her defense because she needed her job to pay her rent. She gave him her phone number and asked that he call her because she wanted to meet outside the restaurant to thank him personally.

Their first date was a picnic lunch and Jonathan subsequently discovered that Danielle had paid one of the restaurant's cooks to prepare the dishes. She later confessed that her culinary skills did not go beyond making grilled cheese, and peanut-butter-and-jelly sandwiches. When he'd offered to reimburse her for the lunch, she'd refused and said it was the least she could do to thank him for saying her job.

During their second date, Jonathan had invited her to his townhome for dinner.

After dating for more than three months, their easygoing relationship came to an abrupt halt once Danielle told him she'd been looking at engagement rings; then when he'd told her he wanted them to date for at least six months before committing to a future together everything they'd shared together imploded. Then it was her request that he purchase the handbag for her birthday that spelled the end of everything she'd shared up to that point.

Although she'd told him that they were done, Jonathan hadn't realized at the time that they weren't because he'd unknowingly had gotten Danielle pregnant despite his using protection whenever they'd slept together. Fast-forward nearly two years… Upon receiving her terminal diagnosis, Danielle had wanted him to raise their son because she didn't want history to repeat itself. The last thing she wanted was for Daniel to grow up in the foster-care system, like she had. Danielle hadn't known her father and had been raised by a single mother who'd died from a drug overdose the year Danielle turned eight. With having no known living relatives, Danielle had been placed in the system.

He hadn't given Danielle the birthday gift she'd sought; however, she had given him a gift that while was so shocking, it was also very meaningful that he was still attempting to process it. He was now a father, and his sole focus and responsibility was protecting his son.

At all costs.

Vivienne waited for Micah's reaction when he opened the envelope Jonathan had given her with the photograph of his family's garden statue. She smiled when he mumbled a curse. "Have you seen this?" he asked.

She nodded. Although FGR had an office in the guest-ranch building, she'd decided to drive downtown, where the Fortune's Gold Ranch occupied a floor of office space in the swanky Emerald Ridge office building. It was where, as the CEO of the cattle operation, Micah conducted most of the ranch's business.

"I wanted you to see it before I make copies to hand out to everyone."

Flipping the image over, Micah stared at the printed material on the back of the photograph. "It looks like the Porters had the statue authenticated and appraised, and that means it isn't something anyone could purchase at a company selling lawn ornaments."

"It's definitely quite valuable," Vivienne said, recalling what she'd asked Jonathan. She also thought of the other objects in his home office, which was somewhat of a museum. Although he'd admitted everything he owned was insured, losing a favored item that could not be replaced did not lessen the loss when presented with a check from the insurance company. Especially if it meant a lot to his family. "I'll make enough copies of the photo of the statue to hand out to the ranch hands before I give this back to Jonathan. I won't copy the appraisal because whoever stole the statue doesn't have to know what it's worth."

"You don't have to do that," Micah countered. "I'll have my administrative assistant make the copies when she comes in tomorrow."

She shook her head. "I'd rather do it. There's no need letting what happened to Jonathan, losing a priceless family heirloom, go any further than it has. Especially if the word gets out about the bandana being found at the scene."

Micah smiled. "You're right about that. We Fortunes don't need any more trouble added to what we're going through with an abandoned baby left on the property, then with Poppy getting that anonymous text accusing Garth of being the baby's father."

"That's because I'm always right," she quipped.

There was a twinkle in her brother's green eyes. "And I'm certain you will always remind me whenever I forget."

"Only when you choose to forget, big brother." She pushed to her feet. "I'll talk to you later and please tell Jacinta that whenever all of this craziness blows over, we should get together for a girl's night out."

Micah got up and came around the desk to hug Vivienne. "I'll let her know."

After leaving his office, she headed to a room where there were several state-of-the-art copy machines. Once she was done, she gathered the copies and went downstairs to the parking lot to retrieve her pickup. She wanted to return the photograph with the attached appraisal to Jonathan before going back to the ranch.

She left town and drove to Jonathan's house. Vivienne used the large brass doorknocker fashioned in the head of a lion rather than the bell because she wasn't certain whether Daniel was still asleep. When Jonathan answered the door, he stared at her as if seeing her for the first time.

She extended her hand with the envelope. "I came to give this back to you."

He slowly blinked, then took the envelope. "Are you in a hurry to go somewhere?"

A beat passed, then she said, "Not right now. Why?"

"I just tried a new recipe, and I would like to know what you think of it."

Now, he'd aroused her curiosity. "What is it?"

"Come in and see."

Why, Vivienne thought, did it sound to her like the story of the spider and the fly? That once ensnared in his web, it would be one from which she would not want to escape. And, at that moment she wanted nothing more than to spend time with a man who made her heart beat a double-time rhythm whenever they were together. "Where's Daniel?"

Jonathan opened the door wider, took a step back, and placed the envelope on the entryway table, then stood off to the side as she walked in. "He's still asleep."

Vivienne was aware that the day care's schedule called for the children to take a nap after lunch. It was when they would unwind before continuing the afternoon activities. "What time does he wake up in the morning?"

"This morning, he was up before six."

Vivienne followed Jonathan into the kitchen and stopped short when she saw small dessert glasses filled with what looked like tiramisu. "Is that what I think it is?" she asked, pointing to eight serving glasses.

"Do you like tiramisu?"

She laughed softly. "I love all Italian desserts. It doesn't matter whether it is cannoli, zabaglione, panna cotta, or, of course, tiramisu."

"I'm also partial to Italian cooking, but I've just begun experimenting with their desserts."

"I noticed you have a lot of cookbooks in your office."

Jonathan nodded. "You could say that I am a frustrated wannabe chef. I consider myself somewhat of a foodie, and whenever I travel, I always sample what the locals eat. I just finished making these, so they will have to go into the fridge for at least an hour. You're more than welcome to come back tonight for an Italian dinner, with dessert, and cappuccino."

"Are you certain I won't be infringing on your time with Daniel?"

"Eating dinner is spending time with him. By the way, do you have a shellfish allergy?"

Vivienne wanted to decline the invitation, but couldn't come up with a plausible reason because what little time she'd spent interacting with Jonathan didn't seem to be enough for her to get to know why she'd found herself so drawn to him. What she had to do was not overthink, something she rarely did, and just go with the flow.

"No, I don't. And thank you for the invite. Do you need me to bring anything?"

A hint of a smile lifted a corner of Jonathan's mouth. "Yes. Just yourself."

"What time should I come?"

"Six."

She nodded. "Six, it is. You don't have to see me out."

Turning on her heel, she walked out of the kitchen. Although she'd told Jonathan that he didn't need to escort her out the door, he'd ignored her and followed her. He opened the door and waited until she was seated behind the wheel of her pickup. She noticed he was still standing in the door-way, watching, as she reversed direction and drove away from the house.

As she headed back toward home, Vivienne still could not believe all that had transpired since she'd awoken the day before. It was the first time since assuming the position of forewoman of the Fortune's Gold Ranch that someone working for her had been accused of being a criminal. And as much as she'd wanted to deny it, the evidence left behind connected the theft of the Porter family heirloom to FGR.

However, the supposition that one of her ranch hands could be on the mastermind's payroll paled in comparison with her face-to-face interaction with Jonathan Porter. Everything about the *über*-wealthy oilman radiated power and confidence, and when he'd looked at her, Vivienne felt that he wasn't looking at but *through* her. It was as if he'd known the effect he'd had on her while she'd inwardly struggled to not show how much she was physically attracted to him.

No! It wasn't an attraction.

It was lust!

Vivienne did not want to believe she was coveting a man raising a baby who had lost its mother. Daniel wasn't a year old, and that meant Jonathan was probably still grieving the loss.

In that instant, she made a promise to concentrate on identifying who had stolen the lawn statue, and not its owner. She would share dinner with Jonathan and Daniel as a gesture of goodwill, then continue with her day-to-day existence as it had been before she'd picked up the phone to answer Jonathan Porter's call.

Chapter Four

Vivienne stared at the pile of clothes on her bed. After driving back to the ranch and storing the copies of the photo of the lawn statue in the office safe to distribute the following morning, she had come home to plan what she'd wanted to wear to Jonathan's house.

Why, she thought, was she in such a quandary over sharing a casual dinner in the home of someone with whom she'd had little or no contact in the past? Yes, she and Jonathan Porter were familiar with each other, but only in passing. Now, she was reacting like a teenage girl with a crush on a boy who'd asked her out on a date. And, then again, maybe his inviting her to dinner was his attempt to prove he was sincerely sorry for accusing someone from FGR of stealing his lawn statue without ample proof? Not only had she accepted his apology, but she'd also agreed to come for dinner.

Vivienne returned skirts and dresses to the walk-in closet. She'd decided to wear a white poet blouse with slim-cut white jeans. She hadn't wanted to put on anything that revealed too much skin, or what she thought of as seductive. Although donning boots, jeans, and man-tailored shirts were the norm for her, there were occasions when she decided to wear something she deemed a bit more feminine. She stared down at her bare feet, frowning. The rose-pink polish on one of her big toes had chipped, and that ruled out wearing sandals; she was past due for a mani-pedi. After searching through a few boxes, she selected a pair of white tennis shoes.

Glancing at the electronic clock on the fireplace mantelpiece, Vivienne knew she had to hurry if she wanted to shampoo and then blow-dry her hair and make it to Jonathan's house on time. If she had one pet peeve, it was tardiness. As she walked out of the bedroom and into the en suite bath, Vivienne reminded herself once again that going to Jonathan's house was *not* a date. He'd simply extended an olive branch, and she'd accepted it. There were enough past and present family feuds in Emerald Ridge without the Fortunes starting up one with the Porters. A spat with a Porter was certain to impact Jonathan's sister's relationship with Nash, where their son Colt Fortune Porter would no doubt be caught in the middle.

So, if going to Jonathan's house was an indication that things were better between them, then Vivienne wanted to reciprocate and invite Jonathan and Daniel to her home on the Fortune's Gold Ranch as a gesture of friendliness, and to support him as the police worked to solve the case of his family's missing heirloom.

She shimmied out of her robe, then stepped into the shower stall, and turned on the water to the programmable temperature. Humming under her breath, she wet her hair, and added a dollop of shampoo, thinking how differently this evening would end when compared to the others she'd had in the past. Different because it would be the first time she would have dinner with a single father.

"Please stop pushing my hand away, Daniel, because Daddy needs to brush your hair. We're having company, and I know you don't want Vivienne seeing you look like you don't care about your appearance. Girls like well-groomed boys, and it's not too early to start now."

Jonathan had found himself carrying on monologues with Daniel when he knew the child didn't understand what he was saying. However, he wanted to expose him to as many words possible that he would eventually understand and be able to repeat.

It had admittedly been a trying day for them both. His baby boy had woken from his nap in a bad mood. He'd sprayed Jonathan before he was able to exchange his wet diaper for a clean one, and wouldn't stop crying until Jonathan picked him up. He'd tried humming to him, but even that hadn't calmed the baby. It wasn't until he'd taken him downstairs and gave him one of the teething rings that he kept in the fridge that Daniel finally stopped crying. It was apparent cutting teeth was painful. As a new father, Jonathan had found himself at a disadvantage. Because it wasn't just that he didn't know anything about babies—he hadn't known until a few days ago that he had even fathered a child, and that meant he had had to a lot of catching up to do.

Earlier that morning, he'd gone online to order a few books on babies and childcare in the express hope that he would become more attuned to what Daniel wanted and needed. His son wasn't walking or talking yet and that meant it had become a guessing game. Although Vivienne had admitted that she didn't have children, she'd made it look so easy when holding Daniel and getting him to calm down enough to fall asleep.

Maybe his sister was right when she'd suggested he hire a nanny, but when he had given it some thought, relinquishing Daniel to the care of a nanny wasn't what Jonathan needed to get to know his son. He'd been denied the first eleven months of Daniel's life, and that was something he wouldn't be able to get back. However, going forward, he'd pledged to do everything within his power to make up for the past and hopefully give their child the best life possible.

Jonathan set the brush on the vanity and shifted Daniel so he could see in his image in the mirror. "See how handsome you are, little man? Now, you're ready for company."

He had bathed, groomed, and dressed Daniel in the hope he would appear presentable, but Jonathan wasn't certain whether it was the same for him. At least not emotionally. It was as if he'd invited Vivienne to dinner without thinking about it beforehand. His offer had just come out and it had been too late to retract it. And she would be the first woman, other than those in his family, whom he'd invited into his home.

Why Vivienne Fortune, he thought, when there was still the possibility that someone connected to her ranch could be responsible for stealing his lawn statue?

He was not one to normally second-guess himself, but if Jonathan was being honest, then he would have to admit that he liked Vivienne. Liked her the way a man liked a woman. Daniel also liked her, and the score was two in favor of the Porters.

Jonathan carried his son downstairs to the kitchen and placed him in a playpen in a corner because he needed to keep an eye on him when cooking. He'd taken the salesperson's advice about childproofing and had purchased electrical outlet covers and heavy-duty magnets to prevent a child from opening a cabinet with cleaning supplies. Fortunately, for now, Daniel was content to sit in the playpen and bang on a stainless-steel bowl with a wooden spoon. He'd thought about Vivienne mentioning toys to keep a baby occupied. It was something they would discuss over dinner.

He was setting the table in the eat-in kitchen when his

cell phone dinged a familiar ringtone. Jonathan tapped a button, activating FaceTime. "Hi, Imani. How's it going?"

"All's well. I'm just calling to let you know that Mom and her sisters are driving back home tonight."

Jonathan frowned. "I thought you told me they weren't coming back until next weekend."

"That was before she told me Dad called to tell her about Daniel. Now, if you're not ready, then you must get ready for Abena Porter's histrionics."

Jonathan hadn't been there to witness it, but Imani had told him that their mother's reaction to becoming a grandmother for the first time was like witnessing a contestant's excitement on *The Price Is Right*, once told by the host to "come on down!" Between the tears and swooning, Imani had been slightly taken aback that their always prim, proper, poised mother had exhibited another side of her usually staid personality. As the wife of an oil magnate, Abena had made certain to always present herself as a sedate Texas socialite. But apparently, when a baby was involved, all bets were off.

"I think you're being a bit premature. After all, this isn't Mom's first grandmother rodeo."

"I'm just saying that you should be prepared just in case it happens."

Jonathan smiled. "Thanks for the heads-up. Now, when are you coming over so our sons can meet each other?"

"That should happen any day now because Nia is flying home from Paris as we speak. She'd gone there to discuss collaborating with a company who sell made-to-order baby clothes for their elite customers. As soon as she recovers from jet lag, I'll be over to see you." His sister grimaced. "Between running Lullababies and arguing with Grandpa about not wanting to head Porter Oil, there are times when

I don't know whether I'm coming or going. But once she's back, I'll have more time to concentrate on Porter Oil."

Jonathan knew Imani's priority was Lullababies. Her business was an extremely successful boutique specializing in one-of-a-kind specially designed babywear. Nia had agreed to take over the boutique during Imani's maternity leave, then they would subsequently run the boutique together with Nia taking the lead, but her unexpected trip to Paris had left Imani with the sole responsibility until their cousin's return to the States.

"Don't argue and upset Grandpa about taking over Porter Oil here in the States."

"Why not, Jonathan?"

"Now that I have Daniel it's going to be impossible for me to divide my time working here and overseas. You can take his place on the board, while I'll manage the day-to-day operation."

There came a long pause before Imani said, "Are you telling me that you're thinking about staying in Texas and leaving Dad to run things in Dubai?"

"It's not what I'm thinking, but planning. And once I discuss it with Dad, I'm certain he will agree with me. Don't forget, whenever I'm in the States I always conduct overseas business remotely. And once Daniel's older, I'll take him with me. But right now, that is not an option. What Dad needs to do is convince Mom to get on a plane and spend some time with him."

"I agree. That wouldn't be a problem if Mom didn't hate flying."

He sighed. His sister was right about their mother not wanting to fly. The one time she'd been forced to let go of her fear was when she'd believed that Dad had gotten hurt in an explosion, and she flew to Dubai to be with him.

Thankfully, he was okay. "What she needs to do is get over not boarding a plane unless there is a family emergency."

"You're preaching to the choir, Jonathan. However, that's something she must come to terms with on her own."

"I hear you, sis," he said.

"Well, I'm not going to keep you because you probably have your hands full with Daniel…"

"He *is* a handful," Jonathan admitted, "but I like being a dad."

"Good for you. Nash says the same thing. I'll talk to you later, and good luck with Mom."

"Before you hang up, I need to tell you that someone stole the lawn statue."

Jonathan filled Imani in on everything about the theft, from finding the FGR bandana left at the scene by the thief, to the police retrieving it as evidence. Although he'd initially confronted Vivienne Fortune, accusing someone from her family ranch as the perpetrator, she'd denied it, claiming she'd planned to hand out copies of the photo of the statue to her ranch hands.

"I'm glad you told me about the lawn statue, so when Mom gets home, I'll let her know someone stole it."

"Thanks."

Jonathan ended the call and thought about what he'd said to Imani to calm her anxiety about taking over Porter Oil from their grandfather. Hammond Porter, who headed the board of Porter Oil, had hinted for years about stepping away from the position. Now that his grandchildren were involved in the family business, he'd felt confident enough to have Imani replace him. What their grandfather failed to accept was that Imani wanted to run her own business. That Lullababies was as important to her as oil was to Hammond and his son, Phillip, his grandson, Jonathan, and probably in the future, great-grandson Daniel. There were jokes that it was oil and not blood that ran in Porter veins.

That said, Jonathan knew it would be a long time, if not years, before he boarded the company jet to fly overseas with Daniel. Firstly, his son would have to undergo a series of shots before traveling out of the country. Maybe by the time he was enrolled in school Jonathan would take him to Dubai during school vacations. And that was more than five years away…

He'd just finished setting the table when the chime of the doorbell echoed throughout the house. Daniel stopped banging on the bowl and pulled himself up, holding on to the playpen's railing. Jonathan walked over and scooped up his boy.

"Let's go, buddy. Vivienne's here."

Jonathan opened the door and went completely still. Vivienne Fortune was a vision in white with a flowing, frilly blouse, jeans, and footwear. Her blond hair, parted off-center, was styled in a loose ponytail. He peered closer, noticing she had applied a hint of makeup to her eyes and mouth. Jonathan's entrancement was shattered when Daniel held out his arms for Vivienne to take him.

She walked inside and handed Jonathan a decorative shopping bag, then took Daniel. Smiling, she dropped a kiss on his head. "How's my handsome big boy? And you look adorable in your little sailor suit."

Jonathan closed the door, experiencing his second shock in less than a minute. Vivienne had called Daniel "her boy." Had it been a figure of speech, or wishful thinking? Jonathan had grown up believing a child needed both parents in their life.

He'd watched the adoring love and longing stares, the barely perceptible intimate caresses between his parents when they'd believed their children weren't watching. It was something Jonathan had wanted to experience with his wife, who would become the mother of their children. However, it was too soon to begin to thinking about a wife or a mother for Daniel when the week before he'd had no inkling that he had fathered a child.

"I know you told me not to bring anything. But, if we're having Italian food, then Leonetti wines will go perfect with what you're serving."

Jonathan peered into the bag and smiled. Leonetti Vineyards had earned the reputation of producing award-winning wines for more than a century. "Thank you very much."

"So, you're not angry with me?"

Jonathan's smile faded. "Why would I be?"

"Because you told me not to bring anything."

He wanted to tell Vivienne he couldn't possibly be angry with a woman who appeared to like his son as much as Daniel appeared to be drawn to her. He didn't know if the baby's attraction to Vivienne was because she was a woman and that he missed his foster mother, or if there was something about her that made him feel safe and secure while in her arms.

"No, Vivienne. I'm not angry with you. Besides, this will be a first for me because I've never sampled Leonetti's wines." He'd purchased bottles of domestic and foreign wines for his collection, yet none bore the Leonetti label.

"Then, you're in for quite a treat. When I first saw this house, it reminded me of Leonetti Vineyards because it resembles an old Tuscan villa."

"Really? Because that's actually the reason I decided to buy this place. It reminded me of Tuscany."

"You've done a lot of traveling." Vivienne query was a statement.

"Come into the kitchen and I'll tell you about my travels while I finish cooking. Would you like anything to drink before we sit down to eat?"

She shook her head. "No, thanks. I'll wait for dinner."

"It won't take long. I've prepped everything, so it will take about twenty minutes before everything is done."

"Is Daniel eating with us?"

Jonathan shook his head. "No. I fed him earlier."

Vivienne sat at the cooking island with Daniel on her lap gnawing on a teething ring, watching Jonathan gather the ingredients he'd prepped for dinner. Small bowls with diced shallots, garlic, and finely chopped fresh parsley leaves lined the countertop. There was also a bottle of extra-virgin olive oil, dry white wine, a lemon, butter, salt, and pepper. A clear bowl was filled with large, peeled, deveined shrimp. Jonathan slipped a bibbed apron over his shirt and jeans and tied a bandana over his head. He'd admitted to being a frustrated chef, and with the apron and head covering he appeared to be one. It was apparent that he was used to preparing gourmet meals in his chef-inspired kitchen with all those top-of-the-line appliances.

"I'm going to make shrimp scampi with pasta. Do you want linguine or angel hair?"

"What's the difference?" she asked.

"Angel hair is less filling."

"Linguine, please." Linguine and penne were her favorite pastas. "Now, tell me about the countries you've traveled to," Vivienne said, as Jonathan filled a large pot with water and set it on the stovetop to boil.

"The travel bug hit me for the first time after I'd completed my sophomore year in college. My roommate and a few other guys spent the summer in Rome, Paris, and then

London. We drank wine, roamed the streets at night visiting clubs, and I would occasionally go to museums, where I discovered I really liked art."

She listened, enraptured when Jonathan told her about visiting six of the seven continents while in college and following his graduation. As a jet-setter, he'd lived off the proceeds from his trust fund, taking cooking classes and purchasing artifacts from many of the countries he'd visited.

He gave her a sheepish grin. "My high-flying days, living my life on my terms, ended once my father asked me work with him in Dubai."

"When did that happen?"

"Four years ago," Jonathan admitted, then tested the linguine to see if it was done and drained it into a bowl."

"Do you miss traveling?"

"Believe it or not, I don't. At the age of twenty-eight the wanderlust had waned, because I'd visited every country on my wish list."

"Which country was your favorite?" Vivienne asked.

"It wasn't so much countries, but *cities*. I loved Venice and Rome in Italy. Paris, Marseille, and the Loire Valley were my favorites in France. I also enjoyed hanging out in Dublin, Tokyo, Hong Kong, Sydney, Nairobi, Athens, Lisbon, Bangkok, and Madrid."

Vivienne shook her head in disbelief. "Didn't you get tired of traveling so much?"

"Only when I got homesick, which wasn't that often."

"What about now? Do you still plan to travel?"

Jonathan met her eyes. "I can't, with Daniel. I'm going to wait until he's old enough to be enrolled in school before taking him out of the country."

She managed to hide a smile. If Daniel was approaching his first birthday, then that meant Jonathan would remain stateside for the next five years. And a lot could happen in five years. Maybe there was some hope for her that she and Jonathan could become friends, or…

Hold on! Vivienne knew she had to rein in her traitorous thoughts before she found herself in over her head emotionally. What had been an initial spark when she'd come to Jonathan's house for the first time was now an out-of-control fire that only sleeping with him could quench.

Initially, she had told herself it was because she was undergoing a sexual drought that Jonathan Porter had made such an impact on her. He was the first man with whom she'd been physically attracted to in a very long time. But now, she knew that wasn't the only reason she was so drawn to him. His gorgeous face and body aside, it was also his willingness to embrace his status as a single father. Jonathan had given up jet-setting when his father asked him to become involved in the family's overseas business, and now he had stepped back from that because being a dad to Daniel had taken precedence. It was obvious his loyalty to his family was always a priority.

Vivienne was more than aware of what it meant to work hard to maintain the Fortune's Gold Ranch. She had sacrificed having a love life while she'd learned all she could to become forewoman. Then, she'd been too busy to date because she didn't want a relationship to interfere with her responsibilities to the ranch. It had taken her five long years to achieve her goal, and now she was ready for the next phase of her life—to embrace a relationship with the right man.

The problem was, there weren't any men she'd wanted to spend time with, but then Jonathan had become the exception. He hadn't come on to her, and he wasn't googly-eyed that he had hit the jackpot because her last name was Fortune. Plus, she knew he could not ignore the bond Daniel was forming with her. She was becoming quite fond of the child, and it wasn't wishful thinking that she could one day become the baby's stepmother, because in all her happy-ever-after fantasies, children had not figured into the equation. And it still intrigued her why she hadn't thought about motherhood.

"How did your lawn statue become a Porter family heirloom?" She'd asked Jonathan the question so he would continue talking and she could stop thinking about him.

Jonathan smiled as he melted butter in a large skillet, then added shallots, garlic, and red-pepper flakes. "That goes way back to my great-grandfather, Solomon Porter. Although he'd come from a long line of blacksmiths, he'd fancied himself a collector. His wife said he was nothing more than a junk man, but that didn't bother Solomon. He wasn't as famous as Charleston, South Carolina's Philip Simmons, but his wrought-iron work was exceptional. He was commissioned to make pieces for a staircase, balcony, and a house gate for a wealthy Dallas banker. Every dollar he earned, he saved, because he wanted to buy land." Turning away from the stove, he briefly met her eyes before returning to the task at hand. "Once his fame spread, he had other customers who wanted him to work for them. One customer who'd gambled away his fortune offered to give Solomon the Zen master meditating statue in return for payment. He accepted the statue and stored it away in his workshop. He'd all but forgotten about it until he placed it in the yard with all the other scraps he had collected, and the next day when he went outdoors, he discovered the ground was covered with what he'd believed was black mud. What confounded him was it hadn't rained the night before."

"It wasn't mud, but *oil*," Vivienne said, her eyes sparkling with excitement.

"Yup. Solomon had discovered there was oil under the vacant parcels he'd been purchasing over the years to add to his initial seventy acres. And the rest was history, with the beginning of what would become Porter Oil. Solomon thought of the statue as his lucky charm and decided it was to be passed down through the next generations of Porter men on their thirtieth birthday because he'd turned thirty when he first came into possession of the statue."

"Who had it appraised?"

"I did because when I saw one that was similar in a Beijing museum, I wondered if it was authentic or a reproduction. Apparently, the original owner had gone to China before it had become a communist country and brought back a lot of art pieces and pottery. And because the statue wasn't listed as stolen, it will remain in the Porter family. That is if the police can identify the thief and we can get it back."

"Will you put it back on your lawn?"

"Yes, but this time with a tracking device."

"I said before that your office looks like a museum," she pointed out. "You probably should put tracking devices on every piece."

"I'm not going to go that far, Vivienne, because I don't want to live in fear that someone's going to break in. The house security system is monitored, so with the installation of cameras and, if necessary, an electronic fence, this place will have all the protection it will need.

She hoped he was right. Some of the large ranches in Emerald Ridge had become victims of thefts and sabotage, while the smaller ranches, like Crescent Circle, Double C, and the Hampton Verde, hadn't reported any incidents.

"Is there anything I can help you with?" she asked. "I feel guilty sitting here watching you cook."

"You can put Daniel in his high chair, then fill the water

glasses from bottles in the fridge. There's also a wine-chiller sleeve in the freezer that will cool the wine in minutes. You brought the wine, so you can select which one you want to drink."

Vivienne smiled. It was apparent Jonathan had opted for a wine sleeve rather than a bucket when chilling wine. She wondered what else the international businessman would do to surprise her.

His home was filled with priceless objects. He'd admitted to being a frustrated chef. He was affluent and wasn't known to flaunt his wealth. The Porsche was the only indication that he'd had enough money to purchase a vehicle with a six-figure price tag. And as an eligible bachelor, he had not become a subject for gossip, because if he'd been with a woman then neither were apt to kiss and tell. Although she had never seen him with a woman, he'd had a relationship resulting in the birth of a child. A child whose mother had died, leaving Jonathan to raise their son. Daniel was an adorable little boy who, unknowingly, had Vivienne thinking about the possibility of one day becoming a mother.

She still had time—time to find the man with whom she would fall in love and have a family together. Vivienne knew if she'd mentioned to her mother that she was thinking about making her a grandmother, Darla would begin planning to turn one of the empty rooms in her wing of the Fortune's Gold Ranch mansion into a nursery that would rival those of members of a royal family. Having a baby was possible if she was able to conceive. But having one with Jonathan was pure fantasy on her part because she'd believed work and his son were his priorities.

Not love.

Chapter Five

Vivienne thought she was eating in a fine Italian restaurant after she'd swallowed a mouthful of perfectly seasoned al dente linguine and succulent shrimp in a sauce flavored with garlic, shallots, and white wine.

"Oh my gosh! This is *so* good." She smiled across the table at Jonathan. "Kudos to the chef. I think you missed your calling because you should've gone to culinary school."

"I appreciate the compliment." He stared at Vivienne over the rim of his wineglass before setting it down beside his plate. "But that isn't an option because I'm expected to work for Porter Oil. Cooking is, and will remain, a hobby."

"What about when you retire? Have you thought that it could become your second career?"

Jonathan smiled, bringing her gaze to linger on his mouth and making her wonder how it would feel if he kissed her. *Get a grip!* Vivienne did want to believe that she was sitting at Jonathan's table and fantasizing about him kissing her when the man hadn't done or said anything to indicate that he was remotely interested in her.

"Fifty years from now, I'll probably still be involved in running the company. My grandfather is in his eighties and only now is talking about stepping down as head of the board of directors."

"Are you going to take over from him?"

Jonathan shook his head. "No. I've talked it over with Imani and she'll head the board in Chatelaine, while I will monitor the day-to-day operation of the outpost here in Emerald Ridge."

Vivienne lowered her eyes, staring at the tender white asparagus wrapped in prosciutto and dusted with Parmesan cheese Jonathan had grilled as a side dish to the scampi. Hearing him say he was staying in Texas buoyed her hope that… Again, her thoughts trailed off. Why was she reading so much into becoming involved with Jonathan Porter, when their only connection was his stolen lawn statue? Once the crime was solved, then there wouldn't be a reason for them to have any further interactions.

"I suppose Porter Oil is like the Fortune's Gold Ranch. Once in, it's impossible to get out."

Jonathan laughed loudly, startling Daniel, who'd dropped his teething ring. "You sound like Michael Corleone in *The Godfather Part Three*, when he says 'Just when I think I'm out, they pull me back in.'"

It was Vivienne's turn to laugh. "You're right," she agreed. "Ranching is in my blood. My father would sit me on a horse in front of him whenever he went out to inspect the cattle when I still wasn't old enough to attend school, despite my mother throwing a hissy fit that if something were to happen to me, then she would never forgive my father. I still can remember telling him to make the horse go faster, but Hayden Fortune wasn't about to incur the wrath of his wife if I was injured as the result of a riding accident."

"How old where you when you were allowed to ride by yourself?"

Vivienne scrunched up her nose. "I think I was either seven or eight. And I was never allowed to go riding alone. My father always had one of the ranch hands accompany me."

"Do you like ranching?"

She smiled. "I love it. Even after so many years, I'm still in awe of watching a calf being born, standing up, and taking its first steps. Granted, it took me a while to get used to the smell of cow manure as a child, and when I complained to my father that I didn't want to go into the barns because of the odor, he explained that manure equaled money because it was sold as fertilizer. And everyone knows that Hayden and Garth Fortune are not only competitive, but both cousins are obsessed with making money."

"That's where the Porters differ. There is no competition among us."

Vivienne swirled linguine around the tines of her fork. "That's because Porter money is considered new when compared to the Fortunes, who date back to the late 1800s."

"We definitely are new money," Jonathan agreed.

She wanted to tell him not only were the Porters wealthy, but it was also purported that they may have had even more money than the Fortunes. "What I like is that you don't flaunt your wealth."

Jonathan's eyebrows lifted slightly. "This house isn't what most folks would think of as a starter home."

"How big is it?"

"Six thousand square feet with six bedrooms, eight bathrooms, set on five acres."

"Had you planned on purchasing something this large?" she asked.

"No. I would've been content with three bedrooms and two baths on a half acre. But once the Realtor showed it to me, and I fell in love with it and couldn't resist putting in an offer."

"Did you have to negotiate with the owner?"

Smiling, Jonathan shook his head. "No. In fact, the sale went very quickly. The owner had moved back to Italy to try and convince his fiancée to come to Texas with him once they were married. He'd commissioned an architect to design the house as a wedding present for her."

Placing an elbow on the table, Vivienne rested her chin in the palm of her hand. "And I assume he couldn't convince her?"

"That is correct. She was under the assumption once they were married, they would live in Italy, while he'd presumed because she came from a humble working-class family, she would be willing to live anywhere if they were together."

"How pompous of him!"

"Well, his arrogance got the better of him. He listed this house with a Realtor, married his girlfriend, and is now living with her in Italy."

"Talk about karma," Vivienne mused. She clapped her hands and Daniel, who had been watching her, did the same as he let out a squeal. "You see, Daniel agrees with me."

"That's because Daniel likes you."

"That's because he knows I like him."

Jonathan gave Vivienne a long, penetrating stare. His son liked Vivienne and he also like being around her. It was as if she was a ray of sunshine, brightening everything around her. He was aware their initial meeting had been fraught with anger and accusations, but now that cooler heads had prevailed, Jonathan was willing to adopt a wait-and-see stance to see what the police would uncover about the theft of the heirloom statue. He'd apologized for his hasty remarks, and inviting her to his home for dinner represented a peace offering.

"Once you bought this house, was it turnkey?"

Vivienne's question stopped Jonathan from admitting to her that he, like his son, liked her. "No. I'd met with an interior decorator and told her that I wanted the furnishings to reflect the interior of homes in a Tuscany village. I was flying back and forth between the States and the Middle East, so we had to communicate electronically. She would send me photos of different pieces for my approval, and whenever I was in Texas I would meet with her to view the rooms that were completely furnished."

"How long did that take?"

"About eighteen months. Once the interiors were completed, then I wanted to concentrate on the exteriors."

"Can I see it?"

"See what, Vivienne?"

"The outside of your house," she murmured.

"The sun is setting, so you won't be able to get the whole picture," he told her. "You'll be able to see it whenever you come back again."

"Are you inviting me back?"

A slight frown furrowed Jonathan's forehead. "Why *wouldn't* I invite you back? After all, you're not the thief who stole the lawn statue." The instant the last word slipped off his tongue, Jonathan knew he'd put his foot in his mouth. "I'm sorry, Vivienne. I shouldn't have said that."

"You're sorry, Jonathan?" Her blue eyes glimmered with anger. "You always apologize, then when you issue more insults and accusations, before apologizing again. And I'm getting tired of hearing them."

After pushing back his chair, Jonathan got up, rounded the table, and stood before Vivienne. Cupping her elbow, he gently pulled her up from her chair until they were facing each other. He was aware that only inches separated them, and he was able to inhale the intoxicating scent of roses clinging to her hair, feel the whisper of her breath through parted lips against his jaw, and see the rapidly beating pulse in her throat.

"I am sorry."

Vivienne's eyelids fluttered wildly. "I don't believe you because you say it—"

Jonathan's head dipped and he stopped her words, while capturing her lips with his own as he kissed her. The kiss ended as quickly as it began when he pulled away and saw Vivienne staring at him like a deer caught in the blinding glare of a vehicle's headlights.

He wanted to apologize, but then he did not want to repeat what she was accusing him of spewing—an endless string of apologies—but he hadn't known what possessed him to kiss her. Perhaps self-consciously, it was something he'd wanted to do since meeting her. That it was her beauty, feistiness, connecting with Daniel, and the knowledge she wasn't a gold digger that had appealed to him as no woman had in his past.

"I shouldn't have done that."

Vivienne's heart was beating so fast she suddenly felt lightheaded. She hadn't expected Jonathan to kiss her, and seconds before it ended, she'd wanted to kiss him back. "Why did you?"

"Because you wouldn't stop talking. And truth be told, kissing you has been on the back of my mind all night. I couldn't help myself."

Her eyes flared. "Is that so?"

"Yes."

"Is that what you do to other women to stop them from speaking?" she demanded. "Kiss them?"

"Not other women, Vivienne. Just you."

"What's next?" she asked breathlessly. "Sorry, not sorry?"

"No, Viv."

"Don't you dare call me that because you haven't earned the right not to call me by my given name."

A slow smile flitted over his handsome features, adding to her ire. "What do I have to do to earn that right?"

She felt as if she was running an emotional race with Jonathan—one that she had no chance of winning. Vivienne knew she was treading into deep water with no way to get back to shore, where sanity and common sense would allow her to make rational decisions. If she'd been sensible, then she should've pretended to be insulted that Jonathan had given in to his impulses and kissed her.

"Trust me and don't insult my intelligence. I told you before that I'm not your enemy. I want to uncover who is responsible for the thefts and vandalism as much or even more than you." Swallowing hard, she briefly met his eyes before continuing. "After I hand out copies of the photo of your statue to the ranch hands tomorrow, and if they all deny knowledge of it, then I plan to go to the jail to talk to the prisoner who is awaiting sentencing to see if he's willing to give up the second thief, or even mastermind."

"I can't let you do that!"

Vivienne wasn't certain whether she heard panic or anger in Jonathan's voice. "Do what?"

"You can't go and talk to someone who has been charged with a crime."

"Why not, Jonathan?

"What I mean is that you shouldn't go alone. If you're determined to play detective, then I'm going with you."

"Why? To play good cop, bad cop?"

"No. It will be Team Fortune and Porter."

Vivienne's expression brightened. "So, we'll become tag-team partners."

"Yes." He paused. "But there's a problem when it comes to Daniel. I'm going to have to get someone to look after him. Imani has promised to come over when she gets a break, so I'd like to wait for her to get here."

"We don't have to wait for your sister," Vivienne told him. "You can always leave Daniel at the Fortune's Gold Ranch's day-care facility for a few hours."

Jonathan shook his head. "Right now, I don't feel comfortable putting him in day care."

"You're not enrolling him, Jonathan. It's just for a few hours. The facility has a wonderful staff who will take good care of your son. It would be the same if you left him in the care of a trusted babysitter."

"Give me a day or two to think about it?"

She nodded. "Okay." The prisoner wasn't going anywhere anytime soon, so a few more days would not make much difference. "And speaking of Daniel, he looks as if he's falling asleep." The child's head was bobbing up and down, then without warning, he appeared to wake up before his eyes closed again.

"I'm going to take him upstairs and put him to bed," Jonathan said, then turned and walked to the high chair and gently lifted the infant out.

"I'll take care of everything here," Vivienne volunteered.

"You don't have to do that. I won't be long."

She ignored him as she began clearing the table of plates and serving pieces. It was the least she could do after Jonathan had prepared a restaurant-worthy meal. For years, she'd thought of her dinner host as a bit of an enigma. She'd noticed him from afar and had been intrigued by him, but had been too cowardly to approach him and ask how he was doing. She was a Fortune and he a Porter, which made them social equals, yet unlike his sister, who had become involved with a Fortune, it wasn't the same with Jonathan.

There was always gossip in Emerald Ridge surrounding its inhabitants, yet there was little or no talk about Jonathan, except that as an international businessman there were occasions when he was rarely seen in nearby Chatelaine or the Porter Oil outpost in Emerald Ridge. It had been the same once he'd purchased his home. He was there and then he wasn't. However, all the speculation as to the whereabouts of Jonathan Porter would soon end because when he'd returned to Emerald Ridge this time around, he wasn't alone. He had come back with a son.

Well, now they were Team Fortune and Porter. Although she still planned to go to the jail to talk to the thief, she was glad Jonathan had offered to accompany her. Hopefully they could convince the man it was in his best interest to reveal who had hired him to target ranchers and a private residence.

Despite yawning and rubbing his eyes, Daniel wrestled against going to sleep. Then he began crying. "You know you're tired, buddy, so why are you getting so upset?" Jonathan asked him in a soothing voice, hoping it would calm the child.

The poor little guy had had a trying day, and now, although he was obviously tired, his son didn't want to go to sleep. Not only did Daniel keep Jonathan on his toes, where he had to be on constant alert to keep things off the floor so the baby wouldn't put them in his mouth, but he also demanded a lot of attention. He would cry if he couldn't see Jonathan, and occasionally spit out food he didn't like.

Daniel's nighttime routine was a warm bath and a bottle of milk, but Jonathan had altered it because he'd given his son a bath before Vivienne arrived for dinner. And he was even having second thoughts about giving him a nighttime bottle. At eleven months old, his son was able to hold and drink from a sippy cup, and drinking from a bottle seemed like his development was going in reverse.

There was so much Jonathan didn't know about babies because there wasn't a definitive manual on how to become a good parent, since every baby was as different and unique as a set of fingerprints. But what he had to learn through trial and error was how to gauge Daniel's moods until he was old enough to talk and tell him what he wanted, liked, or disliked.

But parenting woes aside, he wouldn't trade what he'd found with this little boy for anything in the world. He had only picked up his baby boy from the lawyer's office yesterday, yet Jonathan realized the moment he'd held his son, everything was different. *He'd* become different. That the little boy was completely dependent on him was a huge responsibility, but he would do right by him no matter what it took.

He was finally able to get Daniel to stop crying. Breathing a sigh of relief, Jonathan watched his son staring up at him as he sucked on a pacifier. "No more bottles at night, okay, buddy? You're a big boy because you can drink from a cup. Bottles are for babies." Daniel smiled around the pacifier in his mouth. "I know you understand what I'm saying. Yes, you do," Jonathan continued with his monologue when the child laughed.

"I know you like Vivienne and I like her, too. She is

what I think of as very, very special, so I must be careful not to hurt her." Jonathan watched the rise and fall of Daniel's chest, and believed he had scored a tiny victory. His son had fallen asleep without a bottle.

Pulling a lightweight blanket over his legs, Jonathan adjusted the room's thermostat, turned off the light, and walked out. Several night-lights illuminated the nursery in a soft calming glow. He took a lingering glance around the room. Vivienne was right. Aside from the crib and changing table, it was much too sterile for a baby's development.

He descended the staircase and walked into the kitchen. Vivienne had cleaned up the kitchen when he'd told her not to. It was as if he'd been talking to the wall. Headstrong, determined, and demanding, Vivienne Fortune was so very different from any other woman he'd known that he found himself slightly off his game with her. One thing he could not forget was that she was a Fortune. She came from an *über*-wealthy Texas family going back countless generations. As a cowgirl-turned-ranch-forewoman, she was as formidable as she was beautiful. She didn't take orders. She *gave* them. She was the boss on the Fortune's Gold Ranch, while he was the boss of his home, and he didn't need a woman to take over his kitchen.

His kitchen had become his happy space, and he wasn't ready to share with anyone. It was where he was able to live out his fantasy as a chef while adding or replacing ingredients in popular recipes. The kitchen was his sanctuary, where he was totally at peace with himself and the world. He'd found himself temporarily forgetting about Porter Oil, remote and in-person business meetings, and the unsettling effects of jet lag on his body's circadian rhythms. Jonathan would synch his cell phone's playlist to the speakers concealed throughout the first floor and listen to show tunes and movie soundtracks while he chopped, minced, and blended the ingredients for a selected dish.

Jonathan wanted to reprimand Vivienne for ignoring his orders, then changed his mind. He'd done enough damage when he'd caught her off guard by kissing her earlier. Although he'd admitted to her that he shouldn't have done it, inwardly, he hadn't been sorry. Sitting across the table and watching her eating, he hadn't been able to pull his eyes away from her mouth. Vivienne Fortune had been blessed with perfect lips that some women paid thousands to plastic surgeons to achieve. It was when she'd had launched into a mini tirade about his apologizing that the fragile thread on his entrancement with her snapped and he had gotten up, and rounded the table to kiss her. In that split second, when his mouth covered hers, Jonathan realized what he'd felt was so right had become so wrong. He'd tasted her mouth and wanted more, while he'd chided himself, saying it could not happen again.

"Thank you."

Vivienne's head popped up as she stopped wiping the breakfast island's countertop. "For what?"

Jonathan forced a smile. "For cleaning up the kitchen."

"You cooked, so I didn't mind cleaning." She set down a sponge. "I'd like to do it again, and next time you and Daniel can come to my place for dinner."

"You cook?"

Vivienne's delicate jaw dropped. "Of course, I cook! Who do you think feeds me?"

"I thought you'd have a private chef."

"It's apparent you know nothing about me," Vivienne said, her eyes narrowing and reminding Jonathan of a Siamese cat that had attacked him when he'd attempted to pick up one of her kittens.

He sat on a stool, facing her. "I must admit, I don't."

"Maybe it's time I school you, Jonathan Porter. I'm not some spoiled little rich girl who spends her time shopping, or having lunch with other rich women who spend most of their free time being pampered at their favorite spa. I've worked hard to become the forewoman of a prosperous cattle ranch, and I can ride, rope, and shoot as well as any of my brothers or ranch hands." She huffed out a breath. "And once I turned twenty-one, I moved out of my parents' house and into my own cabin on the ranch. My brothers and cousins also live in their own cabins on the ranch."

"So, in other words, you really didn't move away from home," he teased, grinning.

"I live far enough away from my parents, brothers, and cousins where all of us are afforded complete privacy from one another."

"Are you saying you can't spy on your brothers and cousins, and they can't see who's creeping around to visit you?"

"Men I'm involved with don't *creep*, Jonathan. They are invited. And for your information, Luther Vandross's 'Creepin'' happens to be one of my favorite songs.

He lifted an eyebrow. "You like Luther Vandross?"

"Don't look so shocked, Jonathan. I'm partial to ballads and Luther Vandross, Michael Bublé, and Sam Smith are some of my favorite male vocalists."

Vivienne was right. Jonathan didn't know that much about her, and because he'd found her intriguing, he wanted to know more. "Are you currently involved with someone?"

"Yes," she admitted, smiling. "He's a little young for me, but I find myself unable to resist him."

"How young, Vivienne?"

"Quite young."

Jonathan was shocked, unable to believe a thirtysomething woman would resort to getting involved with a much younger man. Was it maternal or a power trip, because as a forewoman she was used to wielding a great deal of power over the ranch hands?

"I believe you're familiar with him," Vivienne said, meeting his eyes. "His name is Daniel Porter."

Waves of shock were replaced with relief once Jonathan admitted to himself that he was jealous of Vivienne's so-called much younger suitor. That he had been lying to himself that his attraction to her went beyond a mere liking. Vivienne had met the proposed criteria he'd once created for a woman. It was something he'd felt necessary because he was so tired of gold diggers who were after his money. Vivienne didn't want or need his money, and it wouldn't matter to her if he had been disinherited because he was his family's black sheep. Her involvement wasn't with him. It was Daniel.

"My son?"

"Yes, Jonathan, your son. I may come to your home to talk about the thefts, but it is Daniel I really want to see."

Well, damn. I can't believe I would have to compete with a baby for the attention of a woman whom I've struggled to ignore...and failed miserably. Well, Miss Vivienne Fortune, in case you didn't know it, I'm going to have to tell you that Daniel and I are a matched set. You can't have one without the other.

"So, you have a thing for my son?"

Leaning over, Vivienne brushed her mouth over his. "I have a thing for the father *and* the son," she whispered.

Jonathan half rose off the stool, to increase the pressure of her mouth against his. "Now, we're even." He'd kissed her, and now *she'd* kissed him.

Vivienne rested her forehead against Jonathan's. "Now, the fun begins."

"How much fun are you thinking about?" he asked gruffly.

"That depends on you, Jonathan. Right now, the ball is in your court."

"Are you willing to give me time to come up with some strategy as to how you want to play this game?"

"Take all the time you need," she whispered, running her finger down the bridge of his nose, "because you know where to find me…"

Jonathan could not have imagined inviting her to dinner would turn into a sensual cat-and-mouse game he wasn't certain he was prepared to act on. He'd been aware of something simmering between them the instant Vivienne walked into his home, yet at the time he had chosen to ignore it, because it was the first time he'd felt something pass between them that he'd never experienced with any other woman.

Vivienne Fortune had the advantage in the game they were about to play because she was confident of the effect she had on him and his son. Karma had turned the tables on him once again. Vivienne Fortune, and not Jonathan Porter, would determine how their relationship would proceed.

"I don't know about you, but I'm ready for coffee and dessert."

Cradling her face in his palm, Jonathan kissed her cheek. "One cappuccino and tiramisu coming up for the beautiful lady."

Chapter Six

"Why do you look like you've been up all night?" Drake asked Vivienne when he met her for the ranch hands' morning briefing. "Maybe you should send your boyfriend home before the sun comes up."

Frowning, she landed a soft punch on his shoulder. "I wasn't with a man. I couldn't sleep because I was thinking that once we hand out the copies of the photo of Jonathan's statue, one of our people could turn out to be on the mastermind's payroll."

Vivienne had lied to her brother. It wasn't the theft of the Porter heirloom that had kept her from a restful night's sleep, but the man to whom the statue belonged. They'd traded kisses, albeit chaste ones, yet it had conjured up a fantasy in which Jonathan was making love to her. Several times during the night, she'd woken from an erotic dream that left her moaning as she waited for the flutters between her thighs to subside. Once she was back in control, she feared going back to sleep and remained awake until the sky brightened with the hint of a new day.

"Let's hope you're wrong," Drake countered.

Vivienne wasn't certain why she'd always felt closer to Drake, who had been adopted by her parents as a newborn, than she did with her biological brother, Micah. Maybe because they were only a year apart and she thought of him as her twin because they both had blond hair and blue eyes.

She read off a list of works in progress and more repairs on her to-do list, while stressing that replacing the roof on the breeding barn was a priority. Then, she said, "Before I dismiss everyone, I need to report that there has been another theft." Murmurs and curses followed her announcement. "This time it was at Jonathan Porter's home."

"I thought the thief only targeted ranches," a man called out.

"That was before Jonathan became a victim," Vivienne said. "Drake is going to hand out a copy of a photo of the item that was stolen off the Porter property, and if anyone has seen it, the police will need to know. I've been told that law enforcement is planning to come to the ranch to talk to everyone because evidence belonging to this ranch was left at the scene." She had deliberately avoided mentioning the statue.

"What the hell is this thing anyway?" Drake had just handed the assistant cook a copy of the photo of the lawn statue.

"It is something that's personal for the Porters." Again, she'd decided not to disclose what the statue had been appraised for.

Vivienne watched Drake as he distributed the photocopies. All the men shook their heads, and few laughed, saying who would want to steal something looking like that.

"What do you think?" she asked Drake once everyone had been dismissed.

"I don't believe any of our people are involved in the thefts or sabotage, let alone a statue that's worth hundreds of thousands of dollars. Once the police come and talk to each one of our employees individually, we'll know for certain that our folks are in the clear. Speaking of Jonathan Porter, is it true that he has a baby, or is having one?"

Vivienne was suddenly taken aback by Drake's question. "Why would you ask me that?"

"I'm asking because Micah overheard someone in the office talking about seeing Jonathan in the baby store ordering furniture. We know it's not for his sister, because she has what she needs for Colt."

It was said that gossip traveled faster in Emerald Ridge than a streak of lightning. Vivienne knew it was useless to lie because not only had she been to Jonathan's house, but she had also met Daniel. "He does have a son, and he's raising him alone because the baby's mother passed away."

"Oh man! That can't be easy, especially for Jonathan, who's so used to traveling back and forth between here and the Middle East."

"He told me that he's going to stay in Texas until Daniel's ready to go to school."

Drake stared at her with wide blue eyes. "You've met his son?"

"Yes. And he's adorable. He looks exactly like Jonathan."

"That's trouble for these guys who have daughters because when the girls grow up, they will have to be placed on house arrest to keep them away from Porter's son."

"What are you talking about?" Vivienne asked, frowning.

"I ran into Jonathan Porter a couple of time at social events and women were practically salivating over him. It was worse than an old Tom Jones concert, where women tossed their panties at him, and he would wipe the sweat from his forehead before throwing them back."

Vivienne smiled. She'd recalled watching old-school

music videos with Drake when they lived at home. "How did Jonathan react to them?"

"He was always polite and didn't appear to be affected by all the attention directed at him. Porter was different from some of the dudes I've known who are doubly blessed with wealth and exceptionally good looks, because he'd always treated women with respect. Let's hope he'll raise his son to be as much of a gentleman as his father."

Vivienne had grown up around men all her life, and that included having close relationships with her cousins, Rafe and Shane, as well as her brothers, Micah and Drake, and it was a rare occasion when she'd overheard them issuing a glowing compliment about another man. And to her, that made Jonathan Porter special in her eyes.

He may not have accepted overtures from the women Drake had observed him with, yet there had to have been someone exceptional enough for him to date, sleep with, or even marry, and who had given birth to his son.

"I'll call Jonathan later to let him know that no one on the ranch has seen his statue."

Drake dropped an arm over her shoulders. "I keep thinking who's next. Who is going to be the mastermind's next victim?"

"Whoever it is, Drake, he should be very careful, because there is no such thing as the perfect crime. One mistake and the whole house of cards will come tumbling down."

"We'll just have to watch and wait."

Drake was right. Watch and wait, though she didn't mention that she and Jonathan planned to pay a visit to the accused thief before he was sentenced and transferred to a state prison.

* * *

Jonathan had just ended his conversation with the security company scheduled to install cameras on the property when the doorbell rang. Imani had sent him a text message earlier that morning to let him know their mother and aunties were coming over, and she planned to introduce Colt to Daniel later that afternoon.

Daniel, who had been sitting on the kitchen floor, was suddenly alert and began crawling toward Jonathan. It hadn't taken long for the boy to connect the bell with the door. Scooping him up, Jonathan kissed his forehead.

"Now, it's time for you to meet your grandma and great-aunties Mazie and Yemana."

Fortunately, Daniel was in a much-improved mood than he'd been the day before. He woke around seven, succeeded in feeding himself fistfuls of Cheerios, and drank all his milk. His boy had even opened his mouth wide when he'd fed him pureed pears, clapping his hands and laughing once Jonathan said, "All gone."

Jonathan had discovered Daniel was content to sit and watch him whenever he changed the crib bedding, disposed of the soiled diapers in the Genie, and put up loads of laundry. He would talk to Daniel, saying "Daddy has to wash your clothes or make your lunch," because he wanted his son to get used to hearing language.

Jonathan unlocked the door and shook his head when Abena let out a scream that startled Daniel, prompting the child to grab the front of his shirt and begin crying. "Mom, please. Tone it down."

"Sorry...didn't mean to scare him." Abena appeared to be in shock when she stared at her grandchild. "I just can't believe he looks exactly like you when you were his age!"

"I'm certain you didn't have to take a DNA test to determine if you are the father, because he's your spitting image," Mazie said, grinning from ear to ear.

Yemana cackled her distinctive laugh. "I used to watch *Maury* when he'd open an envelope with the results of a DNA test and announce 'You are the father!'"

Jonathan shot his aunt a death stare. He wasn't about to tell her about his relationship with Danielle, because she always had an opinion about everything and everyone.

"Where's his mother?" Yemana asked.

However, in that instant, he'd wished he'd told his *mother* everything about his relationship with Danielle so she could stop her sister from prying. "She passed away after giving birth to Daniel."

Suddenly, a pall enveloped the space as Jonathan met his mother's eyes. "Oh my, I…" Her words stopped when she put her hand over her mouth.

Jonathan realized Abena was becoming emotional. "I don't want to be rude, but it's time for Daniel's nap and I'd like to keep him on schedule, so I'd like everyone to leave and come back at another time that's convenient for all."

His mother lowered her hand. "Jonathan's right. All of us don't need to come at the same time because Daniel seems to be overwhelmed." Going on tiptoe, she kissed Jonathan's cheek, then Daniel's tearstained one. "I'll call you and we can set up a time when I can come and spend time with my precious grandson," she whispered. Turning on her heel, she ushered her sisters out the door, which Jonathan then closed and locked behind them.

Using his thumb, he swiped at Daniel's tears. "I know, buddy. That was even too much for me. How about you and I take a nap together?" Daniel buried his face against Jonathan's neck, still whimpering. It had only taken a few days for his son to get used to a calm and quiet environment, and that's the way he'd wanted to keep it. That said, he'd given Vivienne's suggestion some thought about leaving Daniel at the day care, and concluded a couple of hours in the company of other babies was doable.

Jonathan opened the door, smiling when he saw his sister with Colt on her hip. Imani handed him his nephew, along with a large colorful shopping bag and a diaper bag while she took Daniel.

"He's so precious, Jonathan. And you're right. He looks just like you."

"There's no denying he's mine. Daniel's all Porter while Colt's genes had compromised with those of Porter and Fortune." His nephew had large hazel eyes.

Imani tucked her hair behind one ear to put it out of Daniel's grasp. "I don't know why babies love to pull hair. Most times I must pin my hair up because whenever Colt grabs a handful, he doesn't want to let go. There are some outfits from Lullababies and a few little baby things for Daniel in the shopping bag. There're also bottles of milk and water for Colt in the diaper bag that must go in the fridge," she said, without pausing to take a breath.

"Colt likes hair and Daniel goes for the nose. Let's go to the kitchen where we can talk while we feed the babies." Jonathan had decided to make mac and cheese; he'd spooned out portions for the boys, and put them in the food processor.

"What on earth are you feeding your son, Jonathan?" Imani asked. "He's so much heavier than he looks."

Jonathan smiled proudly. "That's because my boy is all muscle."

"And what is *my* boy?" Imani asked, obviously upset.

"Don't get your nose out of joint, sis. You must remember that Daniel is older than Colt."

"Not by that much."

"Four months is a substantial gap when it comes to a child's development. Daniel will be a year old by the time Colt turns eight months. And my son will probably be walking when yours will be at the stage when he can pull himself up to stand."

"Well, look at you," Imani crooned. "It sounds like my brother has been doing some research on baby development."

Jonathan settled Colt in Daniel's high chair. "I was forced to because I'm clueless when it came to babies. Everything I've ever attempted before came easy. But not so with fatherhood. Every day becomes a challenge where I must be laser-focused when it comes to Daniel." He opened the diaper bag and put the bottles in the fridge.

"So, you like being a father?"

"I'm learning what it *means* to be a father. Right now, it's trial and error. The first time I put on Daniel's diaper it was backward. It's taken getting sprayed a few times for me to remove the soiled diaper and cover him with it before attempting to put on a clean one. I'm also learning how to gauge his moods. He doesn't like being left alone, so I bring him with me when cooking or putting up loads of laundry. I also take him outdoors and we will occasionally nap together in the hammock."

"It looks as if you're getting the hang of being a parent."

"Parenting is not born but learned."

"Talking about parents… Mom told me you were upset because she came over with her sisters."

"I wasn't as upset as Daniel was. He's not used to have so many people around him at the same time."

"Colt's different," Imani murmured as she sat on the

banquette and set Daniel next to her. "He's around people all the time, especially when Nash's family comes over. It took a while for me to keep the names of all the Fortunes straight."

"That's because there are so many Texas Fortunes. Speaking of Fortunes, I want to give you an update on our missing lawn statue..."

Jonathan told Imani that he and Vivienne were working together to try to uncover the culprit and see if it was related to the theft at the Emerald Ridge ranches.

"And you still believe her when she says that no one at FGR is responsible?"

Jonathan met his sister's eyes. "Yes, I do. I must admit I had my doubts until she asked me to give her a photo of the statue so she could make copies to gauge her people's reaction."

Imani frowned. "And she said no one acted like the guilty party?" Jonathan nodded. "Wasn't the man vandalizing the ranches locked up before our lawn statue went missing?" she asked for the third time. Jonathan nodded again. "That could only mean there's more than one thief still out there."

"That's what Vivienne and I want to uncover once we go to the jail to talk the man who's been charged and awaiting sentencing. We're hoping now that he knows he's going to serve time in prison, he will reveal who hired him."

"You and Vivienne Fortune?"

"Yes, Imani. Me and Vivienne Fortune."

"Ah, sookie, sookie."

"What are you sooking about?" Jonathan asked.

"Are you aware, big brother, that every time you mention Vivienne Fortune's name, I detect something in your voice that tells me you and the lady will end up in bed together in the near future."

Jonathan set one dish of mac and cheese on the high-chair tray for Colt and another on the banquette table. He exchanged seats with Imani and settled Daniel on his lap to feed him. "That's not going to happen because I have no intention of getting involved with a woman even if she isn't a gold digger."

"I hope you're still not on that gold-digger nonsense," she said to Jonathan, as she picked up a spoon and fed Colt the mac and cheese.

"No, but using it allowed me to weed out the ones looking to get rich quick."

"Are you certain every woman you dated was a gold digger?"

"Most of them. Danielle had become the exception." Although he'd told Imani he was dating Danielle, the two women had never met each other.

"I remember you telling me that you met her when she was waiting tables at the restaurant where you usually conducted your business meetings."

"She did it part-time to pay her roommate's portion of rent after she'd moved out. She was working at a small law firm while taking online paralegal courses because she eventually wanted to become a lawyer. We didn't get to see much of each other because of her busy schedule. And because I really wanted to see her more than one weekend a month, I told her she could move in with me so she could stop waitressing."

"She turned you down?"

"Yes. She said she wanted to see if she could make ends meet on her own. That's when I realized she was someone with whom I could potentially have a future with."

"But you broke up with her."

Reaching for a napkin, Jonathan cleaned Daniel's face

before going back to spooning creamy mac and cheese in his mouth. "She broke up with me." Jonathan knew he'd shocked his sister when he told her about the argument between him and Danielle that ended with her walking out of his life because he'd refused to give her an engagement ring, and then an expensive handbag. "I don't know if she knew she was pregnant, and that was the furthest thing from my mind because there had never been a time when I didn't use protection whenever we slept together."

"And because you'd refused to propose, she decided not to tell you she was carrying your baby."

"I suppose it was her way of punishing me."

"We'll never know for sure, but if it had been her intent to punish you, wouldn't it have been with a paternity suit that was certain to embarrass the family?"

"I don't know what Danielle was thinking or planning." He told Imani what he'd read in Danielle's medical records. "What she did was compromise her health to carry Daniel to term."

"You can't beat up on yourself, Jonathan. There is no way to know whether she would've survived even if she had terminated the pregnancy. What she did was sacrifice her life for a child who would live on in her."

"You're right, Imani. Although Daniel isn't quite a year old, he reminds me of Danielle's stubbornness because he will throw a tantrum because he doesn't want to nap. And if I allow him to stay up, then he ends up falling asleep and won't eat dinner."

"Stubbornness can be a positive or a negative personality trait. It depends on when it's in someone's best interest to exhibit it."

"You're right, sis. I know you used to get on me about not wanting to date gold diggers, but don't forget you'd considered marrying a parasite before you finally came to your senses."

Imani smothered a groan. "I was hoping you wouldn't bring that up."

"What? That Simon Evans wasn't after your money when he offered to marry you because you wanted a father for your unborn child."

He knew Daniel eventually would need a mother in his life while Jonathan knew he wasn't ready to make that a reality. His past dating history had made him wary of women and now even more guarded. He didn't want to repeat Imani's scenario when she'd agreed to marry Simon Evans to give her son a father. When the time came when he would be faced with choosing a woman to marry, and she became a mother to Daniel, she would have to be willing to accept him and his son.

"Does Colt eat applesauce?" he asked Imani once she finished feeding him.

"He eats everything. What about Daniel?"

"He can have everything except peaches. Sweet and mashed potatoes, creamed spinach, and carrots are his favorites. After I cook them until they are soft enough to puree in the blender or food processor. This morning, I made grits with scrambled eggs, and it was if I couldn't feed him fast enough."

"What about meat?" Imani asked.

"I made sloppy joes yesterday and added it in a dish of mashed potatoes and he loved it." He gave her a curious look. "Why do you ask?"

She grinned. "Well, I need to know what to feed him when he comes to the ranch for a sleepover with Colt."

Jonathan shook his head. "You're really a glutton for

punishment if you're talking about looking after two babies who still can't walk or talk."

"You're the newbie, Jonathan, while I've had a head start when it comes to taking care of a baby."

"What happens if both want to be picked up?"

"That's what hips are for. I'll carry one on each hip."

He laughed softly. "I suppose you are way ahead of me."

Imani made a sucking sound with her tongue and teeth. "Suppose? Please, brother. You know I'm way ahead of you and will always best you when it comes to having children."

"Are you talking about having another baby?"

"Nash and I are considering growing our family once Colt's older."

Jonathan couldn't even think about more children when he'd just discovered he was a father. "This is not a competition, Imani. You, Colt, and Nash are a family, while there's just me and Daniel."

"You and Daniel are a family. However, there is going to come a time when Daniel will need a mother."

"That time isn't now. Please come and sit with Daniel while I get the applesauce." Jonathan had deftly changed the topic because he didn't want to talk about finding someone to step into the role as Daniel's mother. Given his past track record with women, there was no doubt he probably would strike out again. But then he thought about how Vivienne had bonded with his son. Could she... His thoughts trailed off because there was no way he could see himself becoming romantically involved with her when he had to concentrate on raising Daniel.

Imani exchanged seats with her brother. "The next time I come over I'll bring Colt's high chair, so he won't have to hijack Daniel's."

"You don't have to do that. I'll go online and order another one. After the boys finish with dessert, we can have our dinner."

Once Daniel and Colt were done eating, Jonathan placed them in the playpen in a corner of the kitchen. At first, they regarded each other with long stares, but when Colt began crawling, Daniel followed, reaching for his cousin's leg.

"Do you think they understand each other?" Imani asked after swallowing a mouthful of mac and cheese. Colt and Daniel were babbling and occasionally squealing as they engaged in a game of chase.

"Who knows," Jonathan said, smiling. "It's good that they are getting along."

"What's good is this pork. It's goes perfect with the mac and cheese."

"I'm glad you like it because it's my first time trying out the bacon-brown sugar pork tenderloin recipe."

"It's delicious. You know you missed your calling, brother. You should've become a chef."

Jonathan's fork halted over a portion of stir-fried green beans on his plate. "You know that wasn't going to happen when I was expected to get involved in Porter Oil."

Imani touched a napkin to the corners of her mouth. "It took you six long years before you decided to step up and take your rightful place in the company because you didn't want to stop traveling. Meanwhile, I was hearing it from Dad and Grandpa that I had get involved in Porter Oil when we both knew I'd wanted to start my own specialty baby business."

Jonathan winked at Imani. "Everything worked out because I did stop globetrotting to assist Dad in Dubai."

"What you did was stop being a tourist. Flying between here and Dubai is still jet-setting."

"The difference is it's for business and not pleasure."

"Are you going to miss it?" she asked quietly.

"Miss what, Imani?"

"Not flying back and forth between here and the Middle East."

Shaking his head, Jonathan said, "It doesn't matter whether I do or don't, because of Daniel. He's my priority even more so than Porter Oil. The business has survived all these years and will continue regardless if I'm involved. I'll set up a hybrid schedule where I'll divide my time working from home with going into the Emerald Ridge office."

"What about childcare for Daniel?"

Jonathan thought about Vivienne's suggestion they leave Daniel at the Fortune's Gold Ranch day-care center. "I still have time to make a decision about that."

"How much time?"

"It will have to be before the end of the month," he answered.

Daniel would also celebrate his first birthday before the end of the month, and Jonathan was in a quandary. His bond with his son was growing stronger with each passing day and he didn't want to think of the time when he would be forced to leave him in the care of strangers, even if it was only for several hours a day. Leaving him at the FGR day care while he and Vivienne visited the jail would be the first test where he would be separated from his son, whom he'd come to love with all his heart.

"Now that Nia's back and running Lullababies, I'm planning to take a couple of weeks off to spend more time with Colt. You're more than welcome to drop Daniel off at the ranch so they can play together."

"Thanks, sis." Jonathan glanced over at the playpen, noticing that Colt had fallen asleep, while Daniel sat watching him. He knew his son needed to be with other children rather than with an adult 24/7. "Let me know what you want me to bring when it comes time to drop off Daniel."

"Just pack up his clothes and shoes. I have everything imaginable I need to care for a baby. Nash bought enough disposable diapers in sizes ranging from newborn to toddler pull-ups, and squeaky toys that I'm constantly picking up off the floor."

"But you love it, don't you?"

"Yes," Imani said, laughing. "I wouldn't have it any other way."

Jonathan agreed with his sister. Although he hadn't planned to become a father at this time in his life, he, too, wouldn't have had it any other way. It was no longer about himself; it was about Daniel and only Daniel. Every decision he made was based on how it would affect his son.

"I'm going to pass on coffee because it's now past Colt's bedtime and he gets cranky when he doesn't get enough sleep."

"The next time you come, weather permitting, I'll grill, and we'll eat outdoors."

"That's a bet." Imani gathered Colt and her diaper bag at the same time Jonathan picked up Daniel. Together they made their way out of the house.

Jonathan, holding Daniel, watched Imani as she settled Colt in his child safety seat, before she started up her SUV and drove away. "Bye-bye," he said, waving, and Daniel pantomimed opening and closing his tiny fist. He pressed a kiss on his son's curly hair. "I'm so proud of you because you played nicely with your cousin. Colt's going home to sleep, and because you're such a big boy, Daddy is going to let you stay up a little bit longer to see what Auntie Imani brought you."

He returned to the kitchen carrying the shopping bag

with the distinctive Lullababies logo and sat on the floor with Daniel. He removed items that included shirts, shorts, vests, and jackets tailored in exquisite, imported cotton and linen. Imani had also included a yellow rubber ducky and a nubby red ball. Jonathan squeezed the duck, which emitted a quacking sound that had his son in hysterics. Reaching for the rubber toy, Daniel put it in his mouth, biting the beak. Pushing off the floor, Jonathan picked up Daniel, who held on to the duck.

"Let's go, big boy. It's time for your bath and ducky can join you."

After giving Daniel his nighttime bath and settling him in his crib, Jonathan retreated to the kitchen. Between taking care of his son, and entertaining his mother, aunts, sister, and nephew, he was now looking for some alone time. He loved his family yet there were occasions when they were overwhelming whenever everyone got together. In that instant, Jonathan realized he'd become so used to not sharing himself or his time with a lot of people.

While in Dubai it had been him and his father, and the onsite office staff. Even when he'd returned to the States, his day-to-day interactions were with his administrative assistant. She fielded his telephone calls, scheduled his meetings, and kept him sane when she constantly reminded him of the time differences when electronically communicating with the office in Dubai.

He'd promised his father that he was taking a month-long paternity leave before he resumed working for Porter Oil. He'd used one week, and he had to make the best of the next three before the end of June.

He made quick work of cleaning up the kitchen, as he thought about Vivienne. He'd kissed her, and she'd kissed him.

No apologies needed.

Chapter Seven

Vivienne knew she's surprised her mother when she'd called asking to share breakfast together. She'd always marveled how Darla Fortune managed to appear so serenely chic regardless of the time of day. Her dark, lightly streaked, coiffed hair ended inches above her shoulders, and framed a face that belied her age. Darla, in her early sixties, could easily pass for a woman at least ten years younger.

Her mother looked stunning in a pale pink linen blouse and cropped pants. The pearl studs in her ears matched the strand around her smooth neck. "Are you okay?"

Vivienne kissed Darla's scented cheek. "Good morning. And, yes, I'm okay."

"I only asked because it isn't often that I get to see my only daughter anymore," her mom said over her shoulder, as she walked in the direction of the kitchen.

"Now, you're being a drama queen. We had dinner together a couple of weeks ago."

"A couple of weeks when there was a time when we used to get together once a week."

Vivienne sat at a table in a room off the enormous kitchen set with fragile bone china and sterling serving pieces. It was where her parents usually took their meals now that they'd become empty nesters. Darla only utilized the mansion's formal dining room when entertaining. She watched as her mother uncovered a warming dish filled with fluffy scrambled eggs, strips of crisp bacon, breakfast links, and home fries.

"I hope you're not going to sit here and watch me eat," Vivienne said.

Darla picked up a serving spoon and ladled food onto her plate. "The only time I get to eat like this is when your father or my children decide to grace me with their presence. Otherwise, it is fruit, toast, coffee, or tea."

Vivienne rolled her eyes upward. "Why are you being so melodramatic? You know everyone has been on edge because of the multiranch thefts and sabotage. And don't forget there's still the mystery surrounding Baby Joey's mother." Earlier that year someone had abandoned a baby boy on the Fortune's Gold Ranch doorstep. Her cousin Poppy Fortune, a certified foster mother, had been taking care of the baby until the real mother was confirmed.

"I have a right to be melodramatic when there were rumors that the father of the baby Poppy's fostering might be a Fortune, and that includes my sons and husband. Fortunately, DNA results proved otherwise, but now Micah tells me someone has stolen a priceless statue from Jonathan Porter. When will all this madness end, Vivienne? They lock up one man who's admitted to cutting fences and stealing saddles, and now there're others or a copycat targeting private residences, and deliberately leaving evidence that a Fortune or someone connected with our ranch is responsible. What are the police doing to catch these criminals?"

Vivienne picked up a pitcher and filled a glass with orange juice. "I'm certain they are working on it."

"But how fast are they working? I understand Emerald Ridge doesn't have resources like Dallas does, but we do have enough officers where they can concentrate on finding the person or persons behind what has been going on."

"Jonathan Porter and I plan to go to the jail and talk to the prisoner to see if he's willing to give up the name of the person who'd hired him."

Darla slowly blinked, her coffee cup poised in front of her mouth. "You and Jonathan Porter?"

"Yes, Mom. Me and Jonathan Porter."

Vivienne didn't know why her mother made it sound like she and Daniel's father were romantically involved with each other. It wasn't that she did not *want* to be involved; it was just too soon to think of them becoming romantic. Yes, she was physically attracted to him, yet it wasn't enough to warrant diving headfirst into a relationship with the man. She would have to experience something that went beyond their sleeping together to admit she'd fallen in love.

"Is it true that he's the father of a baby boy?"

"Wow! The Emerald Ridge gossip rumor mill is truly working overtime."

"It is true, Vivienne?"

"Yes, Mom. It's true. And his son is adorable."

"You've met the child?"

"Don't look so surprised," Vivienne said, smiling. "Yes, I've met Daniel. After all, when Jonathan called to tell me that the person who'd stolen his family's heirloom had left our FGR bandana behind, I had to go to his home and talk to him."

"Where's the child's mother?"

"Jonathan told me that she passed away."

Darla rested a hand over her throat. "Oh, how sad. I'm certain it can't be easy for him because of his involvement in his family's overseas operation."

Vivienne wanted to tell her mother that Jonathan had de-

cided to curtail flying overseas until Daniel was old enough
to be enrolled in school, but that would be too much information. "He'll probably work something out with his
family. I'm also certain his sister, Imani, will be a big help
because Colt and Daniel are very close in age—" She cut
herself off in midsentence. "Why are you looking at me
like that?" she asked when Darla gave her a long, penetrating stare.

"You keep saying Daniel and not Jonathan's son. And
the fact that you've also mentioned that he's adorable tells
me you like him."

"I like him a lot."

"Enough to…"

"To what, Mom?"

Darla waved her hand. "Nothing."

"It's *not* nothing. Please finish what you were going to
say."

"Enough to change your mind that one day you just
might give me a grandchild."

Waves of annoyance eddied over Vivienne, and she
forced herself not to get up and walk out of the house where
she'd spent the first twenty-one years of her life. "Have you
asked Jacinta when she's going to give you a grandchild?"

The rush of color suffusing Darla's face matched her
blouse. "Of course not. She and Micah are still newlyweds.
They need time for themselves before starting a family.

"And I'm single. Are you saying you want me to become
a single mother?"

"It doesn't matter nowadays whether a woman is married
or single once she's a mother. After I had you and Micah, I
told Hayden I wanted more children, but after I had a difficult pregnancy and delivery with you, we adopted Drake.

You can decide to have a baby the natural way or adopt. Either way, I don't care. It still would be my grandbaby."

Vivienne felt as if she'd been taking verbal body blows from Darla. She could not remember a time when she'd shared time with her mother that she did not mention she wanted grandchildren. She narrowed her eyes. "Is it because the other women with whom you *do lunch* show you photos of their grandchildren on their phones and you don't have any? Or maybe it is a lot closer to home. Are you competing with Shelley now that her son, Rafe, is stepfather to Heidi's year-old twin daughters? I'm certain Shelley is over the moon about it, in addition to Shane, who'd first granted her grandmother status when he was married and had Brady." She huffed out a breath. "Mother, you must stop competing with these other women who lord it over you because you don't have grandchildren. You have a daughter and two sons in their thirties, and we have time before one of us will make you a grandmother."

"You're angry with me, aren't you?"

"Why would you say that?"

"Because you called me 'Mother.'"

Vivienne reached over and held Darla's hand. "That's because you *are* my mother and I love you. Now, I wanted to talk about something that's not as upsetting for you."

Darla leaned forward, interest lighting her eyes. "Do tell…"

"Well, I've read some of the nominations for the Gift of Fortune Initiative and there were a few that had me close to tears. The first one was from one of Emerald Ridge's principals about a teacher who was recently diagnosed with breast cancer and needs emotional healing and a place to stay at the Fortune's Gold Guest Ranch and Spa. And then there was the nomination for a young mother whose husband has passed away, leaving her a widow with triplets."

Darla rested a hand over her chest. "Oh, how sad. I just can't fathom the number of people who need a break from life's trials and tribulations. I'm so glad Rafe and Drake decided to host the Gift of Fortune again because of last year's success."

Drake and Rafe had recruited her to go over the nominees for this year's Gift of Fortune with them, to select some very deserving person or persons who would be granted a deserving complimentary stay at the guest ranch. Drake, who'd been adopted by Hayden and Darla, and given a life his birth parents hadn't been able to provide, always felt he had to give back. When presented with the initiative, Garth balked, suggesting Rafe, his youngest son, was going overboard with the notion of goodwill; however, he'd finally came around, but only after he'd been convinced that it was good PR for the Fortune's Gold Ranch. Rafe, who had heard about a long-lost Fortune named Wendy, who'd recently married, sent her an anonymous invitation last year. Wendy had responded by saying she and her husband, Beau, had made plans to enjoy the guest ranch in the very near future.

"So am I."

"When are they planning to announce the winner?" her mother asked.

"They've set a deadline for the end of the month." Pushing back her chair, Vivienne stood up, Darla rising with her. "I'm going to run because I have a few things on my to-do list I want to accomplish today."

The older woman rounded the table and hugged her daughter. "Thank you for coming." She paused. "I don't want to sound like a nagging mother when I tell you that you need to take your time and have some fun."

Vivienne knew what Darla was going to say, but asked, "What kind of fun are you talking about?"

"Go out on a date and wear some of those pretty outfits you bought when we when on our shopping spree."

"You know I suck at dating, Mom."

"You wouldn't suck if you didn't nitpick at everything a man does or says. No man is perfect and that includes your father. I've learned to pick my battles with Hayden, and there are times when I allow him to think he won."

"I don't want to fight with a man. And I don't want to pretend he's a winner just to soothe his ego. I need one to treat me with respect and as his equal. Some of the men I've dated either want me to act like the stereotypical dumb blonde, while a few want me to be their sugar mama."

Darla's eyebrows shot up. *"Sugar mama?"*

"Yes. It's the flipside of being a sugar daddy. The last clown I'd gone out with said after our second date he expected me to pay for everything going forward, because he's used to dating sugar mamas."

"No, he didn't!"

"Yes, he did, and now he can look for another woman willing to take care of his wants and needs because I'm not the one."

"I'm so sorry, honey. You'd told me that you liked him."

Vivienne rolled her eyes and made a sucking sound with her tongue and teeth. "I did before he stated that he wanted me to be his ATM." She kissed her mother's cheek. "Thanks for breakfast and as soon as everything goes back to normal, we can schedule our weekly get-togethers."

"Let's hope that's soon."

Vivienne wanted the same. To that end, she'd called the

sheriff's office requesting an update on DNA testing on the bandana and was told there was a backlog at the lab and it would take a while for the results. She'd also asked if she could speak to the prisoner before he was sentenced and transported to prison; the sheriff said that was only possible if the prisoner was willing to see anyone other than his court-appointed lawyer. If he agreed, then he would get back to her.

Now, it had become a waiting game for Vivienne, and she absolutely hated it. She walked out of the house and made her way to where she'd parked her vehicle. Sitting around and twiddling her thumbs was not her MO.

Go out on a date and wear some of those pretty outfits... Darla's suggestion made Vivienne smile as she drove away from the main house. What she'd wanted to tell her mother was there was only man she could think of dating, yet he was off-limits. Jonathan Porter was a single father with a nearly year-old baby who had lost his mother, and she doubted whether he wanted to become involved with another woman at this stage in his life. And unlike her last parasite, he didn't need her money. She'd promised Jonathan that she would decorate Daniel's nursery, and instead of going back to the ranch she headed downtown to the baby store. The ranch hand supervising the crew putting up new fencing had sent her a text asking to meet with her later that afternoon to schedule a timeline for replacing the roof on the breeding barn.

Jonathan was standing in the doorway, holding Daniel, when Vivienne came to a stop in the driveway. She'd sent him a text message telling him she was on her way to bring what she needed to decorate Daniel's bedroom.

She had just stepped out of the pickup when Daniel

began squirming and screaming, and Jonathan was forced to tighten his hold on the baby, or he would've slipped out of his grasp. "Hold on there, buddy. I know you're glad to see her."

Daniel wasn't the only one glad to see her. Jonathan was, too. It'd only been two days, yet it could've been two weeks, and what he hadn't realized was that he missed her. Vivienne had become a constant reminder that he'd missed a woman's company. After his breakup with Danielle, his time spent living and working on two continents had left little room for a relationship. He hadn't dated women in Dubai and when he returned to the States that hadn't become a priority because he'd believed long-distance unions were doomed to fail.

Now that he was back for good and he and Vivienne had declared a truce, he'd felt comfortable enough to invite her into his home. Something he'd never done with any woman who wasn't his family. Then, there were her interactions with Daniel. She appeared to genuinely care for him and there was no doubt Daniel was drawn to her as well.

Vivienne extended her arms. "I'll take Daniel while you unload the trunk and bring everything upstairs to the nursery. Meanwhile, this little munchkin and I have a few things to say to each other." She kissed his forehead. "I hope you haven't been fighting with Daddy when it comes time for your afternoon nap," she whispered. Daniel responded by clapping his hands and laughing. Vivienne also laughed. "We're going to have to talk about this, because naps are good for babies because it allows you to calm down and relax. It's the same with me when I go to a yoga class or meditate. Afterward, I feel more clearheaded to accomplish whatever I need to do."

Jonathan gave her a sidelong glance. "You know he doesn't understand a word you are saying, right?"

"Speak for yourself, Jonathan Porter. I'm the baby whisperer, not you."

"Baby whisperer?"

"Yes! I'm betting if I were to feed him his lunch, then get him ready for his afternoon nap, he won't fight with me."

Jonathan chuckled. "Is this a challenge?"

"Yes. It. Is."

He realized Vivienne was serious when she'd stressed each word. "What's the end prize?"

"If I win, then you'll will have cook dinner for me every night for a week. And if I lose, then I will reciprocate."

"You've got yourself a deal." Smiling, Jonathan crossed his arms over his chest. "Looks like it's game on."

"I hope you don't cry or pout when you lose."

Even if he did lose, Jonathan would not think of himself as a loser, because it meant he would get to see Vivienne every night for a week. "After I unload your truck, I will prepare Daniel's lunch for you." He leaned close to Vivienne and whispered, "You're going to lose."

"Keep running off at the mouth, Jonathan Porter, and I will be forced to decide what I want on the menu each day." She laughed when he pantomimed zipping his lips.

Now, Vivienne knew what her cousin Poppy had talked about when fostering the abandoned newborn left on her doorstep. While Poppy was a newly certified foster mother, interacting with a baby was something entirely new for Vivienne. She didn't know what it was about Daniel Porter that triggered whatever maternal instinct she'd refused to acknowledge, and hopefully it wasn't because the boy needed a mother.

Holding, feeding, and singing to him had filled up an emptiness that Vivienne hadn't been aware she'd had. Her fervent wish from childhood was to grow up and run the Fortune's Gold Ranch with her father and brothers. When she'd left the ranch to attend college, she would count down the days when semesters were over so she could return. And once she graduated, she'd promised herself that she would never leave again. It had taken a lot of hard work to finally convince Hayden Fortune to appoint her as the forewoman of Fortune's Gold Ranch.

Daniel ate all his squash, green peas, and pears, then drank most of the water in his sippy cup. "I can't believe you ate everything," she crooned as she wiped his face with a damp cloth. "You're going to grow up big and strong because you like vegetables."

"That's because I *want* to get him used to eating vegetables," Jonathan said, chuckling softly as he entered the kitchen. "There probably will come a time when he'll only want fries and burgers."

"Is that what happened to you?" she asked, lifting Daniel out the high chair.

"Yup. What on earth did you buy? I thought the toy chest was empty until I attempted to lift it."

"It's filled with toys. Every child needs a jack-in-the-box, a set of blocks, a drum, and a xylophone, and, of course—"

"Oh lord, there's *more*?" he groaned.

"Yup, but I'll let you discover that for yourself when you empty it later."

He rolled his eyes. "Can hardly wait."

"I bet," she laughed. "But right now, I'm going to change Daniel, then put him down for his nap."

"Good luck with that," Jonathan said under his breath.

"You can come and watch if you like."

"Of course, I'm going to watch. It behooves me to keep a close eye on this so-called baby whisperer."

Vivienne walked out of the kitchen with Daniel and waited for Jonathan to remove the safety gate at the foot of the staircase leading to the wing of the house where he'd set up his bedroom and the nursery. He did the same with the gate at the top of the stairs.

She'd witnessed Poppy changing Joey's diaper and had familiarized herself as to what to do. Once that was done, she undressed Daniel, leaving on his undershirt and fresh diaper. Then, Vivienne cradled him to her chest as she sat on the glider, staring adoringly down at him as he sucked on the pacifier. Humming a nameless song, she rocked gently, watching as his eyes closed, and within minutes was fast asleep.

She met Jonathan's eyes as he stood watching her work her magic. Vivienne didn't know whether Daniel had missed his mother holding him, yet the close contact, with her singing or humming, was soothing enough for him to fall asleep in her arms. After pushing off the glider, she put Daniel in the crib on his back and left the room, Jonathan following her.

"Piece of cake," she whispered, going on tiptoe until her head was almost level with Jonathan's.

He stared at her under lowered lids. "Okay. You win. You *are* a baby whisperer."

"Told ya!"

Jonathan reached for her hand, brought it to his mouth, and kissed the back of it. "You don't have to gloat. After Daniel wakes up, I'll go through what you bought... Oh, and how much do I owe you?"

"Nothing, Jonathan."

"Don't tell me it's nothing when it looks as if you bought out the entire store."

"Think of it as a baby shower gift." Vivienne leaned close and brushed her mouth over his in barely perceptible kiss. "Now, will you please put it to rest." He'd stopped her talking with a kiss, and now it was her turn.

In a motion in which she'd hadn't been able to take a breath, Vivienne suddenly found herself in Jonathan's arms, his mouth hungrily covering hers. Without hesitation, she kissed him back with a raw hunger that made her want him more. And the more was for him to strip her naked and make love to her, and assuage the erotic dreams that came when she least expected.

Jonathan did not occupy her thoughts whenever she was involved with her responsibilities as the ranch's forewoman. It was only at night, when she prepared to go to bed, that she realized it would become another endless night of sleeping alone. Even when Drake had teased her about looking as if she hadn't slept because a man had kept her up all night, he hadn't known how close he had come to the truth. There hadn't been a man in her home, but there was one in her head.

However, what she'd refused to ask herself was why Jonathan Porter? Why *him* when she never would've entertained dating him because he'd always appeared so disinterested in her whenever their paths crossed? A smile and a nod was not the precursor to them even exchanging a verbal greeting.

Fast-forward several years, and now that he was stateside, and there was the possibility of their dating, she had to think about Daniel. Not just Daniel, but the baby's mother's death—Jonathan was probably still mourning. Vivienne knew she would never be able to replace Daniel's mother, and if she and Jonathan were able to make it as a couple, she didn't want to. What he'd had with his son's mother would live on for the rest of his life.

The kiss ended with both of them breathing heavily. "If you tell me 'you shouldn't have done that,' I will punch your lights out," she said, smiling.

"There's no way I'm going to admit that. Besides, I need my lights to admire the beautiful woman in my arms."

"Aren't you the silver-tongued devil," she teased.

Jonathan wiggled his jet-black eyebrows. "Why, because I'm telling the truth?" He suddenly became serious. "And because you're the total package, I don't know why a man hasn't put a ring on your finger."

"Maybe it's because I attract the wrong men."

"Do you believe in having to kiss a few frogs before you find your prince?"

"I'm beginning to believe it." What Vivienne couldn't tell Jonathan was that she was beginning to wonder if she'd already found him. Could Jonathan be her prince? Or was she just wishing for the impossible here? "I, uh, almost forgot to tell you that I spoke to the sheriff, and he has to ask the prisoner if he's willing to talk to us."

"When will we get an answer?"

"I'm hoping it's soon. I also checked with the day care and the director is open to caring for Daniel whenever we need to drop him off."

Jonathan rested an arm over her shoulders. "Thanks for reaching out to them."

"You're welcome." She glanced at the clock on Daniel's dresser. "I actually need to get back to the ranch and check on a few things."

She and Jonathan left the nursery, and he walked her to her vehicle. "What do you want me to fix for dinner?"

"Surprise me," Vivienne said. She was certain whatever Jonathan decided to make would be delicious.

Opening the driver's side door, he waited for her to slip behind the wheel. "Are you up to eating Italian again? And can you come over a little earlier?"

"Yes, to both." She blew him an air kiss. "I'll see you later." She was backing out of the driveway when she heard a ringtone indicating she had a text message. She'd left her cell phone in her cross-body bag on the passenger seat. Pressing a button on the steering wheel, Vivienne activated the Bluetooth feature, and grimaced when she looked at the navigation screen and saw Drake's name. He'd left her three text messages.

"What's up, brother?"

"That's what I should be asking you, my sister," he said. "Where are you? I've been blowing up your phone for the past half hour."

"I'm sorry, Drake. I forgot we were supposed to meet to go over the ranch hands' July and August vacation schedule."

"I made up a tentative one for you to review before it's posted."

"Thanks, Drake," she murmured. "I'll look at it as soon as I get back."

"Where are you now?"

"I'm on my way back to the ranch. I had to do a little shopping."

Drake's laugh came through the speakers in the pickup truck's cab. "Shopping for more white shirts to go with your jeans?"

It was Vivienne's turn to laugh. Her closet was filled with several dozen man-tailored shirts and jeans. Wearing the same outfit every day meant she did not have to pick and choose as the ranch's forewoman. It was her work uniform.

"No, smart-ass. I was shopping for baby items."

There was silence before Drake said, "Is there something you're not telling me? That I can look forward to becoming an uncle?"

"Don't be silly," she scolded. "It went to buy something for Jonathan Porter's little boy."

"It sounds like you and Porter are getting close if you're shopping for his son."

"We're *friends*, Drake. Nothing more and nothing less."

"Do you want more than friendship from the man?"

Vivienne was glad her brother couldn't see her because heat had suffused her face, and there was no way she could conceal the flush. "No," she lied smoothly. "We and Jonathan, and the *we* meaning the Fortunes, have both been victimized by thefts and sabotage, and we're planning to visit the jail and talk to the thief, and hopefully he can give a hint as to who'd hired him."

"You're going to the jail?"

"Initially I was going to go alone before Jonathan said he was coming with me."

"I'm glad he's going with you. I'm leaving the office now. The schedule is on my desk. I'll go along with whatever changes you decide to make."

"Thanks, Drake."

Vivienne tapped the button, ending the call. She'd lied to her brother about not wanting more than friendship with Jonathan. She wanted benefits.

She returned to the ranch and met with the foreman of the work crew putting up fencing. The ranch hands had replaced the section that had been sabotaged and had secured a portion that sustained damage during a destructive thunderstorm.

Vivienne overruled the hand when he suggested patching the roof, saying replacing the entire roof would in the long run save time and money. Allocating funds for a new roof meant reviewing the budget for an expense that hadn't been added when the projections were established for the fiscal year.

The day-to-day operation of a ranch was challenging, but Vivienne had learned from the best how to overcome them, because she had been mentored by Hayden Fortune.

Running the ranch was challenging but attempting to figure out her emotions when it came to Jonathan surpassed everything she'd encountered since or before becoming forewoman.

Maybe, she mused, it was time to begin to pull back before she found herself in too deep.

Chapter Eight

Jonathan opened the door and went completely still. He didn't know how Vivienne was able to flawlessly change from a cowgirl in boots and jeans, into an ethereal figure dressed in white who took his breath away. She had paired a long-sleeved, flowing linen maxi dress with matching wedge espadrilles, and had styled her hair in a single braid that fell over one shoulder.

Smiling, she handed him a decorative shopping bag. "I don't know if you've ever had Abuela Rosa Chocolates, so I decided to bring some for you to sample."

"You know you're spoiling me with the local goodies. First, excellent wine, and now, chocolates."

"Delicious handmade chocolate that has been handed down through generations of Gomezes."

Jonathan took the bag and then leaned in to kiss her cheek. *Damn! Why did she have to look and smell so good?* He'd tried and failed miserably to convince himself that Vivienne Fortune was just another beautiful woman he was attracted to. And during the years he'd traveled around the world, he'd admired beautiful women in every size, shape, and color, but the difference between them and Vivienne was his reluctance to get involved with any of them. He was a tourist visiting their countries, and therefore had to respect their culture and customs. But he and Vivienne both lived in Emerald Ridge now…which could be a game changer.

Vivienne gave him a sensual smile. "I like spoiling you because I know I'm going to get a restaurant-quality meal in return."

Reaching for her hand, Jonathan laced their fingers together. "Tonight's different."

"How so?" she asked, staring at his profile.

"Because you're going to be my sous-chef."

She stopped short and would've fallen if Jonathan hadn't tightened his hold on her hand. "Hey! That's not fair."

"What's not fair was you showing me up when you got Daniel to fall asleep so easily."

Vivienne arched an eyebrow. "You don't like losing, do you?"

"I don't think anyone likes losing."

"Where's Daniel?"

"He's in his playpen in the kitchen. I fed him earlier, so we don't have to wait to eat."

Daniel's head popped up when Vivienne entered the kitchen. He crawled over to the side of the playpen and pulled himself up to stand. He let out an ear-piercing squeal as she walked over and scooped him up. "Hi, sweetie." She smile at Jonathan when Daniel rested his head on her shoulder. "It looks like you've lost your sous-chef tonight."

"That's okay."

"Seriously? I didn't think you would throw in the white towel that easily."

Jonathan opened a drawer under the cooking island and took out an apron. "Using Daniel to run interference is not a sure thing, *sweetie*. You can sit and watch me make lasagna. I didn't prep anything in advance because I was planning on you assisting me."

"Perhaps tomorrow."

"We'll grill outdoors tomorrow. I have a rack of lamb in the freezer that needs to be cooked before its expiration date."

Vivienne sat on a stool with Daniel on her lap, enjoying the warmth of his tiny body. She nestled him against her chest. Daniel reached for the pacifier attached to a holder clip on his T-shirt and chewed on it before sucking vigorously.

"How often do you shop for groceries?" she asked Jonathan, watching as he set the ingredients for his lasagna dish on the countertop.

"Not too often. I order perishables and other staples from the Emerald Ridge Grocery, and all my steaks, beef, chicken, lamb, chicken, and fish online from a national meat delivery company."

"Wow. It's like you have your life wrapped up in a nice, neat bow."

Jonathan slipped on the apron, then covered his head with a bandana. He wanted to tell Vivienne if he hadn't structured his life to adhere to a strict schedule, he wouldn't have been the least bit prepared to care for Daniel. Meanwhile, Imani had made it look so easy with Colt. Maybe because she had Nash to help, while as a single father, he'd had to do it all. A few times he'd told himself that he didn't have to do it all alone. That if he'd had a wife, they would be able share the responsibility of raising their son.

Now, there was Vivienne, who had bonded with Daniel almost instantaneously. And that could prove to be a problem if they were to become involved and it didn't work out between them. However, he didn't need to think about the worst-case scenario right now, he reminded himself. Instead, he simply allowed himself the pleasure of watching Vivienne as she gently rocked Daniel until his eyelids fluttered closed.

"Do you think he's down for the count?" he asked her.

"I'll wait until he's fully asleep before putting him back in the playpen."

"If that's the case," Jonathan said, removing another apron from the drawer, "this one is yours. I don't want you to get red sauce on your pretty dress."

Vivienne knew Jonathan had gotten his wish to have her stand in as his sous-chef. While she wasn't opposed to helping him cook, she preferred to watch him work his magic in the kitchen. His every move appeared so precise, so confident. It was obvious that Jonathan Porter was totally in control of everything he did. He'd assumed the role of single father with the same focus that had made him a successful businessman before thirty.

The Porters had been profiled in an issue of *Texas Monthly* and Vivienne couldn't stop staring at the family photo. Jonathan stood ramrod-straight, head slightly cocked to an angle under his Stetson, arms crossed over his chest. His image had radiated power and supreme confidence.

When she'd walked into his home the night he'd called to tell her someone from her ranch had stolen his property, Vivienne had been hard-pressed to connect the man wearing a T-shirt and jeans with the always impeccably dressed businessman. And if she had to choose which version she preferred, then it would have to be Jonathan the single father and not the wealthy oilman.

"How long is it going to take before the lasagna is

ready?" she asked. Judging from the number of ingredients it appeared as if they had to do a lot of prepping.

Jonathan handed her a bandana. "Normally a couple of hours. That's why I'd asked that you come over early."

Vivienne folded the bandana into a headband and tied it on the front of her head. Jonathan stared at her, then burst into laughter. "What's so funny?" she asked.

"Are you channeling Tupac with your bandana?"

She'd tied it in front rather than the back because of the elastic band holding her hair in place before she'd braided it. "You got something against Tupac? 'California Love' happens to be one of my all-time favorite tunes on my cell phone's playlist."

Jonathan winked at her. "We have something in common, then, because I, too, like 'California Love.'"

Vivienne wanted to ask him about Daniel. He was something they both had in common as well. She knew Jonathan loved his son, and each time she held the baby she was aware that a bond was forming where she wanted to become a part of this precious little boy's life. Her mother had complained that she wanted to be a grandmother. And Darla hadn't cared whether the child was the result of a natural birth or an adoption.

What if Jonathan and I decided we wanted to become a family? That would make Darla Fortune an instant grandmother. Then she could stop complaining and brag about having a grandchild.

Vivienne shook her head as if to banish her wishful thinking. Why was she indulging in fantasies when she had always been grounded? What was there about Jonathan that made her revert to an adolescent girl who crushed on every actor and performer gracing the covers of entertainment magazines?

But wishful thinking or not, there was no denying that this man had a lot going for him…

Jonathan was gorgeous and sexy. And when he'd kissed her, Vivienne had forgotten every man who had attempted to kiss her before him.

He was wealthy, and that meant he wouldn't view her as his sugar mama.

He was a single father who had given up traveling internationally to raise his son.

And then there was family loyalty. He'd also given up jet-setting to take his place in the day-to-day operation of Porter Oil.

Family loyalty for the Porters matched the Fortunes. Despite the occasional bickering or competition, they did not hesitate to come together in a time of crisis. And this was, for Vivienne, a win-win.

"Do you really need all these ingredients to make a dish of lasagna?"

Jonathan put his arm around her waist, and her eyelids fluttered as she breathed in his clean, masculine scent. "Yes. When I took a cooking class in Italy, I was overwhelmed when the instructor listed everything needed to make what he'd called the world's best lasagna. I didn't believe him until I tasted it once it came out of the oven. It truly *was* the best lasagna I'd ever eaten."

"I know I'm not going to remember everything once I try and make it myself. Are you willing to give up the recipe?"

Jonathan pressed his mouth to her ear. "What I'm willing to do is invite you over whenever you want to eat it."

Turning her head slightly, she met his eyes. Dark brown eyes she believed could see what she'd attempted to conceal the first night she'd come face-to-face with him. That what she'd admired from afar was more potent in person.

"Is the invitation open-ended or will it have an expiration date?"

A hint of a smile lifted the corners of his mouth. "For you, it's open-ended."

Vivienne was certain he could hear her exhalation of relief. Jonathan stared at her under lowered lids, unaware how sensual she found it. "Thank you."

"I should be the one thanking you for how you've helped me with Daniel."

Vivienne felt as if she'd just been doused with a bucket of ice-cold water. She'd come to believe that Jonathan had invited her into his home because he liked her; however, it clearly wasn't about her. It was how she related to his son.

"You don't have to thank me when it comes to Daniel. I've grown quite attached to him."

"And he to you, Vivienne," he murmured.

"I don't want you to think that I'm trying to replace his mother, because I'm not."

A beat passed. "You couldn't replace her, because you're nothing like her. You're the opposite of Danielle."

Vivienne took off her bandana, struggling not to cry. "I think it's time for me to leave."

Jonathan caught her arm, preventing her from escaping him. "Don't!"

"Don't what?"

Pulling her close, he dropped a kiss on the top of her head. "It's not what you think…"

"How do you know what I'm thinking? Have you added mind reader to your other list of talents?"

"I know you believe I'm using you to help me with Daniel," he rasped. "But the truth is, you're the first woman I've invited into my home and allowed to interact with my son that is not a member of my family. And that makes you very special. Daniel likes you and I like you. A lot."

She swallowed a lump in her throat. "What about Daniel's mother?"

"I don't like to speak ill of the dead because they're not here to defend themselves. The only thing I'm going to say is you're nothing like her."

"Were you in love with her?"

A shadow crossed his handsome face. "I'll admit I was falling in love with her. It ended once I refused to marry her, and that's when she walked out on me. I didn't know she was pregnant, and it wasn't until after she'd passed away from kidney cancer that I found out that she'd had Daniel."

Vivienne chided herself for jumping to conclusions. She'd believed Jonathan had been so love in with his baby's mother that no woman would be able replace her in his heart. "I'm sorry I overreacted. It's just that when you said I was nothing like her, I thought I meant absolutely nothing to you."

Jonathan cradled her face in his large hands. "You are wrong, Vivienne Fortune, because you have no inkling of how much you've come to mean to me. And it has nothing to do with Daniel. It's just that whenever I caught a glimpse of you in the past, you always seemed so unapproachable, and *that's* why I'd always kept my distance."

"Me unapproachable? You never gave me more than a passing glance."

"That's because you were Emerald Ridge's ice princess," he admitted gruffly. "Men said you could freeze someone with an icy stare."

"That's ridiculous! I probably wanted to have nothing to do with them because they were a waste of my time. And those I did date wanted to turn me into a Stepford wife."

"Stepford wives don't ride horses, herd cattle, rope, or drive pickup trucks."

Vivienne laughed. "You're so right." Knowing that he liked and wanted to be with her was enough for now, and she planned to take it day by day. "Now that we're on the same page, it's time we start making this world's best lasagna…"

Chapter Nine

Vivienne felt as if she'd truly become a heroine in a Regency novel. She was a modern-day Elizabeth Bennet, who'd fallen in love with the aloof, and overly reserved, Mr. Darcy. She'd had no idea Jonathan was interested in her, yet he had kept his distance. And when she looked back on it now, she realized it probably was for the best they did not date at the time. Vivienne knew she wouldn't have been mature enough to accept his constant traveling; that each time he left the country she would've imagined him with other women.

She was now spending whatever free time she could take away from the ranch at Jonathan's house. He'd help her put up framed posters of animated characters on a wall in the nursery. An area rug stamped with the alphabet with corresponding animals and objects covered the floor. A trio of stuffed bears and rabbits lined the window seat, and the colorfully decorated chest was filled with books, and a variety of talking and musical toys. Vivienne had selected blue, green, and yellow pastels colors to make the space more inviting.

Presently, she sat on the floor with Daniel, singing as the baby accompanied her banging on his toy drum.

"I'm going to pack his clothes and send him to the ranch

with you because I can't hear myself think," Jonathan said, frowning.

Vivienne realized Daniel had become enamored with the drum when first introduced to it, and now refused to play with any of the other toys. "I wouldn't mind taking him home with me."

"You know I'm just kidding."

"And I'm not," Vivienne countered. "Bringing him to the ranch and exposing him to the calves, puppies, and kittens will be fun…" She stopped talking with her cell phone rang. She got up and picked the phone off the banquette. "Yes, we can. Thank you for calling." Vivienne met Jonathan's stare. "The sheriff said if we can make it to the jail by eight tomorrow morning, the prisoner will talk, but for no more than fifteen minutes."

"That's great news," he said.

"It sure is. If it's okay with you, I'm going to text the day care and let them know we'll drop Daniel off for breakfast."

"Works for me. I'll get him up early and have him dressed when you get here."

"You'll just need to bring a change of clothes and diapers. The center has everything else."

Vivienne wanted to suggest that either she stay over with Jonathan, or he and Daniel sleep at her house, then quickly dismissed the idea. They hadn't reached the stage in their friendship where sleepovers were agreed upon.

"Do you mind if I give him his bath before I leave?" Vivienne asked.

Jonathan shook his head. "No, I don't mind. I'm willing to agree to anything for him to stop that drumming."

"You probably won't do well living on a cattle ranch, where there's nonstop sounds day and night," she teased.

"You're probably right," he said, agreeing with her.

Vivienne knew Jonathan was out of sorts once he revealed he'd had to report the theft of the statue to his insurance company within fourteen days. Like her, he'd hoped the police would've recovered the item or received the FGR bandana DNA test results from the crime lab by now. Maybe then they would be one step closer to uncovering whoever had put the man in custody up to causing trouble at Emerald Ridge's most prosperous ranches, and subsequently, at a private residence.

Daniel started crying when she picked him up and stood. "No more drumming tonight, sweetie. You must get ready for bed because tomorrow you're going on an adventure where you will meet other babies and toddlers." Jonathan left the nursery as Vivienne carried the baby into the bathroom.

Vivienne sat Daniel on the floor of the en suite bath as she half filled the tub. After testing the water temperature, she quickly undressed him and put him in the tub with his yellow rubber ducky. It was her first time giving Daniel a bath and she quickly discovered he liked splashing. Water went everywhere as she washed his face and ears. It went over the sides of the tub and she was drenched by the time she was able to wrap him in a towel and carry him back into the nursery.

Jonathan stood next to the crib; his arms were across his chest. "I came to see if you survived."

Vivienne placed Daniel on the changing table to dry him off. "Barely. He likes to splash."

"I should've told you that before," he said, handing her a diaper, after she'd applied a lightly scented baby lotion.

She chuckled. "Next time I'll be certain to wear a poncho." She finished putting on his jammies and placed Daniel in the crib. "Nighty night. Don't let the bedbugs bite."

When she turned around to face Jonathan, she saw him staring at her like a deer caught in the glare of a vehicle's headlights. She knew she looked a mess with wet hair streaming down around her face, but it wasn't her face he was staring at. It was her chest. Water had soaked her shirt and bra, and the outline of her breasts was clearly visible through the wet material.

The song "Hungry Eyes" from the movie *Dirty Dancing* popped into her head and Vivienne knew if she didn't leave now, she would be throwing herself into Jonathan's arms, encouraging him to make love to her. "I'll see you tomorrow," she said, brushing past him.

She was practically running as she picked up her phone and cross-body, and made it to the door before Jonathan could follow her. She was backing out of the driveway when he appeared in the doorway.

He knows. He knows that I want him to become more than a friend. And it hasn't a damn thing to do with Daniel. I want Jonathan Porter not only in my bed, but also in my life.

Tears filled Vivienne's eyes as she navigated the road she had traversed countless times. She was angry because she'd allowed herself to become attached to a child when there was no guarantee she would have a future with Daniel or his father.

She'd called it wishful thinking because she was a fool to fall for someone who'd admitted to liking and being attracted to her, yet nothing beyond that. She'd come to his home practically every day for a week since his initial telephone call, and looking back, Vivienne wondered if Jonathan was of the belief that she'd used his son to get close to him.

But even though she knew that this could all end in

heartbreak, she couldn't help the way she felt about him. Because, the truth was, Jonathan Porter was everything she'd wanted and needed in a man. He was even-tempered, generous, and overtly gentle with Daniel. He'd fallen in love with a woman who'd made him a father, yet he refused to badmouth her. Jonathan had accused her of spoiling him when, in turn, he'd spoiled her when he prepared whatever she'd wanted to eat.

And recently, he had taken her on a full tour of his house and property. She'd found herself overwhelmed with the spaciousness of the Tuscan villa, which boasted two wings with master bedrooms with dressing and sitting rooms, and guest bedrooms, all with fireplaces and en suite baths. The first floor had a home gym and office, as well as a family room with a large wall-mounted television and home theater system. He'd admitted using the formal living and dining rooms only when he'd invited the entire Porter clan.

The outdoors was an oasis with potted plants, trees, and flowers indigenous to the region, and landscapers had installed a waterfall he was able to control electronically. Vivienne preferred eating in the outdoor kitchen whenever the temperatures went down enough to remain outside for any appreciable amount of time. Sitting and communing with nature had had a calming effect on her.

She had grown up on the Fortune's Gold Ranch, believing it would be where she'd raise her own family and spend the rest of her life. So why was she now struggling to figure why she suddenly felt more at home in Jonathan's house than she did in her own?

Vivienne had regained her composure when she walked into her house and set her bag on a table in the entryway. It was too early to turn in for the night, so she decided to stay up and binge watch a series. After the first hour, she knew she was losing it because this was the third time she'd actually watched the series and had even memorized some of the dialogue. Enough was enough. She turned off the television and went into the bathroom to shower.

Twenty minutes later, when she retrieved her cell phone from her handbag to set the alarm, she noticed a small white notecard. She opened the card and found a folded check and the sales receipt from the baby store. Vivienne read and reread Jonathan's bold script.

Thank you for your decorating services—Jonathan and Daniel

It was apparent he'd found the receipt she'd left in one of the bags and wrote her a check for the total amount. So much for his graciously accepting her gift for Daniel. Vivienne had no intention of arguing with Jonathan about it. She was tempted to simply tear up the check, but then changed her mind. She put the check and notecard in a drawer under a stack of T-shirts. If she didn't deposit it, or if he didn't mention it, then neither would she.

She set her cell phone's alarm an hour earlier than normal. Then placed it on the bedside table, turned off the lamp, and went to sleep.

Chapter Ten

"We'll take my car," Jonathan announced when Vivienne drove up to meet him the following morning.

"And I'll drive," she said, extending her hand for the Porsche's fob. "I called the director at the day care and Hannah Peters is expecting us. And don't worry, Jonathan. If I can drive a tractor and shift gears without stripping them, then driving your luxury car is a piece of cake." She smiled when he dropped the fob on her outstretched palm.

Vivienne opened the door and sat behind the wheel, waiting for Jonathan to buckle Daniel into the child safety seat. Once Jonathan got in and fastened his seat belt, she tapped the button to start the engine, shifted into gear, and backed out of the driveway.

"It purrs like a contented cat."

"I like it."

"I see why you like it." She flashed him a quick grin before returning her eyes to the road. "I'm so used to driving the pickup that whenever I drive a car it feels strange."

"Do you have another vehicle other than the pickup?" Jonathan asked.

"Yes. A royal blue punch buggy."

"Are you talking about a Volkswagen Beetle?" he questioned.

Vivienne smiled. "Yup. I take Blue Bayou out at least once week to keep her juiced up."

"You named your car Blue Bayou?"

"I name all my cars. Don't you?" she asked him.

Jonathan shook his head. "No, Vivienne. My cars don't need a name."

"If I owned this Porsche, because it's gray, I'd call it Silver Bullet." Shifting into a higher gear, she increased the luxury SUV's speed. She gave Jonathan a sidelong glance and saw that he'd fisted his left hand, so she immediately decelerated. In a moment of madness, Vivienne had forgotten that Daniel was also in the vehicle. She drove through the gates to the Fortune's Gold Guest Ranch and Spa and parked close to the building.

"You've never been here?" she asked Jonathan, who was staring through the windshield at the guest ranch's main house.

"No," he said, unbuckling his seat belt.

"If that's the case, then welcome to the Fortune's Gold Ranch. When we come back, I'll give you a tour before we pick up Daniel."

"How many acres does the ranch cover?"

"Only three thousand."

Jonathan didn't want to believe Vivienne had said *only three thousand* like it was three hundred. Even three hundred acres was a lot of land. But, then again, the Fortunes were Texas royalty, their roots in the state going back as far as the late 1800s, when steel magnate Leland Fortune established the ranch. The property had been passed down several generations and now was owned by Leland's bickering great-grandsons, multimillionaire first cousins Garth and Hayden Fortune. Vivienne had admitted that her father,

Hayden, was not only in competition with his cousin Garth, but both were also obsessed with making even more money.

He'd acknowledged the Porters were new money, and while they had attained billionaire status, they'd escaped the competitiveness and infighting many wealthy families had experienced. The closest the Porters had come to a financial squabble was when Simon Evans rejected Imani's offer that he sign a prenup agreement. The greedy man failed to realize that Imani had learned to negotiate business deals before graduating high school. That their father and grandfather had required he and his sister to watch and listen while they conducted business meetings, because there would come a time when they were expected to get involved and eventually take over once Hammond and Phillip Porter retired.

Jonathan knew he was knowledgeable enough to step up now that his grandfather was resigning as the head of the board, because he'd supervised the outpost in Emerald Ridge, where a few Porter-owned oil fields were located over the past four years.

What he didn't feel so confident about, however, was his relationship with Vivienne. His feelings for her had surpassed liking and now were rapidly bordering on falling in love. He couldn't understand how it'd happened so fast.

Jonathan repeatedly told himself it was because of Daniel. That his son needed a mother and Vivienne Fortune was the perfect candidate for the role. But if he was completely honest with himself, he would have to admit Vivienne was perfect for him. He woke waiting for her call to say whether she was or wasn't coming over, and when she said she was, then he was waiting for the doorbell to ring. If Daniel connected the doorbell with Vivienne's arrival, it had become the same for *him*. He enjoyed cooking with her because that was a new experience for him. But it was when they sat at the table eating together that it had truly made him, Vivienne, and Daniel feel like a real family unit.

As confident as he'd like to believe he was... That was a lie, because he knew his self-control was slowly slipping away whenever he and Vivienne shared the same space. Unknowingly, she'd turned him on to the point where she'd become an itch he couldn't scratch. Everything about her had begun to affect him physically, and seeing her breasts through her water-soaked shirt the night before had been the final straw. It was only later, after she'd left, that he realized if she hadn't run out of the nursery, he would've swept her up into his arms, strode across the hall to his bedroom, and made love to her. It had taken hours before he'd been able to fall asleep, and when he woke it was time to get Daniel ready for the day-care center.

He got out, opened the rear door, and removed his son from his car seat. The poor little guy had dozed off during the ride. "It's okay, buddy. You can sleep after you have your breakfast." Daniel still didn't wake up when Jonathan carefully propped his sleeping son against his shoulder and accompanied Vivienne into the lobby of the luxurious ranch spa. She then led him down a wing and into a large room that was the spa's day care.

A young woman met them. She was smiling and extending her arms to take Daniel, who'd opened his eyes and let out an ear-piercing scream. "Don't worry, Dad. He'll calm down after you leave."

Jonathan wanted to ask her whom was she kidding. His baby was screaming and struggling to escape the arms of the strange woman holding him. *This wasn't a good idea.* He never should've agreed to accompany Vivienne to the jail to talk to the prisoner and leave his baby boy at a place that wasn't familiar.

Vivienne handed the woman the bag with Daniel's change of clothes. "Let's go, Jonathan. The longer you stay, the more upset he'll become." She grabbed his arm. *"Now!"*

He clamped his teeth together to keep from spewing curses. Daniel was crying—no, he was sobbing uncontrollably—and Jonathan felt as if he was abandoning his son to the care of strangers who knew nothing about him. Once they reached the car, he got in behind the wheel and started the engine, totally ignoring Vivienne when she slipped in beside him.

"He's going to be all right, Jonathan."

"Please don't say anything, because right now I don't feel like talking."

"Well, I do," she countered angrily. "There are a few things you'll have to learn about children. They are more resilient than you think. I've been at the day-care center when guests leave their kids and some cry because they don't want to be separated from their parents. But when they see the other kids playing and watching cartoons, the tears stop and they become engrossed in whatever activity is going on around them. Once Daniel is fed and when he sees other babies walking and crawling, he'll join them."

Jonathan stared out the windshield as he left the ranch, hoping Vivienne was right. Then he recalled Daniel's reaction when he and Colt had been placed in the same playpen and appeared to chase each other. "This is the first time that I've left him in an unfamiliar place."

"And it won't be the last time. You'll leave him on his first day of school and when you drop him off when it comes time for him to attend college. There will be a lot of firsts in Daniel's life, and like you, he *will* survive."

Jonathan couldn't help but smile. "Did you survive?"

"I did, but I must confess that I did get a little teary-eyed when my folks dropped me off at college. I attended a school out of the state, and I knew I couldn't get in my car and drive home whenever I had a break. I was homesick for nearly a month." She paused. "But once I joined a few on-campus clubs, the girls I met became my sisters. After graduating, we managed to stay in touch with one another. A couple came to the ranch last year for a visit, and I've been invited to more weddings and baby showers than I can count on two hands." She slid him a sideways glance. "Do you keep in touch with your college road dogs?"

"Why do my boys have to be *road dogs*?"

"Didn't you tell me that y'all traveled abroad and spent time drinking wine and roaming the streets at night visiting clubs?" she replied.

"Yes."

"Then y'all were road dogs."

Jonathan dark mood lightened when he laughed, and he found himself temporarily forgetting about leaving Daniel at the day care. To say Vivienne was good for him was an understatement. It was as if she'd become the voice of reason when it came to Daniel. She wasn't a mother, yet it was like she knew instinctually how to communicate with a child. Even one as young as his son.

She talked to Daniel, using complete sentences, and not the gibberish he'd heard some adults use with babies. And his son squealed whenever she got down on the floor and crawled around with him as they played tag. There were also quiet times when she'd sit him on her lap and read from a book of nursery rhymes, with repetitive same-sounding words and phrases.

"Have you thought of what you want to ask the prisoner?" Vivienne asked, breaking into his thoughts.

"No. I've decided to play it by ear. We don't need to play good cop, bad cop because the man has nothing to lose. Although he knows he's facing time in prison, he's still jerking everyone around by only allowing us fifteen minutes to talk to him."

"I can't wait to face this creep," she snapped.

"What are you planning to do, Vivienne? Punch his lights out?"

"I really can't say what I'd like to do to him. The man has wreaked havoc because we lost two valuable horses, and the Wellington Ranch had a large hole cut in their fencing leading them to lose four runaway cattle. Other area ranches reported the theft of livestock and pricey saddles, and this clown decides to have selective amnesia and not name who hired him even after he was caught in the act."

"Now that's he's been sitting in a jail cell waiting to be sentenced, hopefully he's had time to think that being locked away isn't worth his protecting whoever paid him."

"His being behind bars means he couldn't have stolen your lawn statue," she pointed out.

"That's true, Vivienne, but I'm willing to bet he knows who did. The man couldn't have acted alone when stealing horses and saddles. He had to have an accomplice or accomplices."

"We'll find out in few minutes because we're almost there."

Jonathan and Vivienne were given visitor passes, then ushered into a room where the handcuffed prisoner sat a table. An armed deputy stood a short distance away. He and Vivienne had decided she would take the lead because it was her brother who'd gone undercover and had apprehended the man. Jonathan pulled out a chair at the opposite side of the table for Vivienne to sit before taking the one next to her.

The prisoner glanced the wall clock. "I changed my mind about giving you fifteen minutes. I don't feel very generous this morning, so your five minutes starts now. Which one of you good folks would like to go first?"

"Mr. Chance," Vivienne began.

"It's just Chance to you, beautiful. There's no need to stand on formalities, not with me wearing these silver bracelets." He held up his handcuffed wrists.

"Okay… Chance. I know you admitted to the thefts and you're going to prison, but is it worth you giving up at least ten or even twenty years of your life based on your lengthy rap sheet not to tell who put you up to it?"

"What's the loss of a few cows and horses to ranchers who have enough money to replace anything I've stolen?" he retorted.

"You alone couldn't have stolen them, so you had to have had an accomplice. Someone who helped and was also responsible for stealing from me," Jonathan said, speaking for the first time.

"And who are you, hotshot? Her bodyguard?"

"He's my boyfriend, and his name is Jonathan Porter."

Chance slumped back in his chair. "Porter as in Porter Oil?" Jonathan nodded. "Well, well, well. I can't believe I have two rich fat cats in my face this morning." Sitting up straight, he rested both hands on the table. "I am not snitching, not to you or anyone. I was paid too well to keep my mouth shut. And it isn't my fault that you ranchers and oil folks just can't get along."

"What *aren't* you saying?" Jonathan demanded.

"What I ain't gonna tell you is who paid me. Once I do my time and I'm paroled, I will be living the high life far away from here. But I will say is that rich folks who compete with one another are apt to do anything to come out on top. It doesn't matter how much money they have, it's always dog-eat-dog."

"Are you talking about ranchers?" Vivienne asked.

"Hell, yeah. Ain't they the ones with the deep pockets? And that includes you, Mr. Oilman. I heard that your folks have enough money to last them into the next millennium. You may not have horses or cows, but some little birdie told me you own a real fancy house. Some would call it a mansion." He glanced up at the clock. "Your time is up." He stood and the deputy led him out of the room.

"What did you think of that?" Vivienne asked Jonathan once they were back in the car.

"He won't admit who hired him, and he has a thing against folks with money. And he kept talking about ranchers competing with one other."

"It's a known fact the Fortunes and Wellingtons were feuding with one another a long time ago, but that's in the past."

"Still, that doesn't rule out your family, Vivienne."

She shifted on her seat and glared at Jonathan. "What you trying to say?"

"I'm not implying anything, Vivienne, only repeating what Chance said about ranchers competing with one another. Weren't you the one who said your father and his cousin were in constant competition with each other?"

"Yes! But not to the point where they would break the law," she snapped.

"You don't have to bark at me, Vivienne. I'm just trying make sense of what Chance told us."

"He said what he did to mess with our heads. What I can't believe is what's coming out of your mouth, where you are trying to blame the members of *my* family of doing something so heinous. After you pick up Daniel and drive me back to your place to get my truck, I never want to speak to you again!"

Jonathan flinched. While he understood why she was hurt, it wasn't like he had accused Hayden or Garth Fortune of being the mastermind behind the multiranch sabotage. He was just trying to figure out what Chance was alluding to. That, just perhaps, he was speaking in code when he'd mentioned ranchers. And his earlier observation that the prisoner also appeared to have a grudge against people with a lot of money made sense, given that while most of the larger ranches were affected, a few of the smaller ones were spared. At least for now. His home wasn't a ranch, yet that hadn't stopped the thief from stealing his lawn statue. The Leonetti family was wealthy, too, but so far, the thief or thieves hadn't targeted Leonetti Vineyards. However, it was possible they could also be victimized in the future if the mastermind wasn't identified or apprehended.

His intention in sharing his perspective about what Chance had divulged hadn't been meant to hurt Vivienne. But her saying that she didn't want to speak to him again made it abundantly clear that he had. But in his defense, if she hadn't disclosed what he hadn't known about her family's past feuds with the Wellingtons, then it was something he never would have said to her. Jonathan wanted to remind Vivienne it had only been two years since he'd moved from Chatelaine to Emerald Ridge, and was conducting business on two continents, leaving him out of the loop when it came to local gossip and shenanigans. He'd had no interest in anything other than Porter Oil.

But now, with the loss of his family's priceless heirloom, he too had been drawn into the craziness affecting the resort town. If the thefts weren't enough, then there was the mystery behind who was the mother of an abandoned newborn and the possibility that a Fortune had fathered the child.

Jonathan sighed. Well, if Vivienne didn't want him to talk to her, he would grant her wish. For now, at least. Besides, he had to focus on Daniel and plan for his son before the end of his thirty-day paternity leave.

Two days later, Vivienne walked into Drake's office and flopped down on a too-soft sofa. She still hadn't gotten over what had occurred between her and Jonathan after leaving the jail. She couldn't believe he had all but accused her family of being behind the thefts and sabotage.

"You need to throw this thing out or replace the cushions."

Drake came around his desk and sat on a corner. "It's worn out from me sleeping on it."

"You have a house and a bed. Why aren't you sleeping in it?"

"When Micah went undercover, I decided to sleep here just in case something jumped off. By the time he was able to catch the SOB, I'd kind of wore it down."

Vivienne frowned. "It was worn down before you began using it as a bed."

"You're not the only one who has complained about it. I'll look into ordering another tomorrow. What did you and Porter find out when you went to the jail?"

"Not much."

"How much is not much?"

She filled in her brother on their meeting, finishing by saying while she wasn't surprised that Chance refused to name his boss, she was taken aback by his hostile comment about rich ranchers competing with one another, and his insinuation that one of them was responsible for the thefts and sabotage. "It's as if he was angry with people who had a lot of money because he even attacked Jonathan once he discovered he was connected to Porter Oil."

Drake grunted under his breath. "You and Porter got a lot more out of him than the police. Because when they interrogated him, he said he'd been paid too much money to become a snitch. Once he pled guilty, he'd refused to say another word. His pointing the finger at ranchers is what's bothering me."

Vivienne wanted to tell her brother it had been the same with Jonathan. He had even gone so far to suggest that maybe her father or Garth could be the masterminds. But she knew there was no way her father or his cousin would stoop that low to outdo each other. That was beyond incomprehensible.

"How many times did he mention ranchers?"

"I don't know. It had to be at least three or maybe even four times. He talked about ranchers having deep pockets, so it's nothing for them to lose a few cows or horses."

"Do you think it's possible for you or Porter to talk to him again?"

"Probably not, Drake," she replied. "The man has a grudge against folks who have a lot of money even though he claims he was paid well to commit the crimes." She didn't want to tell her brother that she was no longer speaking to Jonathan, so his suggestion was moot.

"That's too bad. Because we really need to catch who-ever is behind this before someone else becomes a victim."

Vivienne nodded.

She wanted to clear the Fortune name as much as any-one. Which reminded her that they were still waiting for the DNA test results from the FGR bandana left on Jona-than's property. She whispered a silent prayer that Jonathan was wrong that a Fortune could be implicated in a crime that would re-create a feud between the ranchers that had taken decades to put to rest.

Jonathan was lying in the hammock with Daniel, his mind in tumult. It had been two days since he and Vivienne had visited the jail, and despite his attempt to replay what Chance had disclosed, he still felt something wasn't adding up. It had something to do with the ranchers, but his gut told him it couldn't have been the Fortunes if Micah had gone undercover as one of the ranch hands and had eventu-ally caught the thief. Why would they have paid the man, then planned to apprehend him? It just didn't make sense.

"Vivienne said she never wanted to speak to me again, but I didn't promise her I wouldn't speak to her," he said to Daniel, who was looking up at him as if he understood what he was saying. "What do you think? Do you think I should humble myself and apologize?" Jonathan smiled when the baby grunted. "Is that a yes?" This time Daniel smiled, showing the two new teeth that had finally broken through his gums. "That's what I like. We're Team Por-ter. I miss her like crazy, and I'm willing to bet that you do too." He reached for his cell phone, and sent Vivienne a text message:

Sorry for what I said the other day. Can you forgive me—
once again? We need to talk.

He didn't have to wait long for her reply.

Yes, I forgive you once again. Please let's not make it a
habit.

I promise it won't happen again.

When do you want to talk?

Anytime that is convenient for you.

How about the day after tomorrow?

Sure. Dinner?

Yes!

What time should I expect you?

Is five too early?

Five is perfect. Bye.

Later.

Jonathan shifted Daniel until he was lying across his
chest. He hadn't expected Vivienne to accept his apology
so easily, but he sure was glad that she had. And this time,
if they were to talk, it had to be about devising a plan to
catch the mastermind before he or she struck again.

Chapter Eleven

Vivienne had suggested waiting a day before seeing Jonathan because she needed to treat herself to a much-needed massage. Every muscle in her body was as tight as a bowstring. She hadn't been able to move without wincing or groaning, and had attributed it to tension.

The truth was, she'd been dealing with a lot of stress ever since Poppy informed her that someone had left a tiny newborn in a carrier on her porch. Her mother, Shelley, and Courtney Wellington were in the house with her when Poppy found a note pinned to the baby's blanket indicating Baby Joey was a Fortune and they should care for him since the mother couldn't. And if there hadn't been enough trouble in Emerald Ridge with someone or a group of criminals stealing and sabotaging prosperous ranches, a young woman named Jennifer Johnson arrived in town insisting the baby was hers, but since the Fortunes had bonded with Joey, she was willing to relinquish all claim to the child for half a million dollars.

Vivienne could not imagine any woman willing to sell her child for money and she knew along with everyone else that Jennifer Johnson was a grifter.

Whether slick or a grifter, Jennifer's DNA test confirmed she was the mother of Baby Joey, which left everyone heartbroken for the baby. What mother would leave her baby on a doorstep, then turn around and demand money? However, she did agree to sign over parental rights and allow Poppy and her fiancé, Leo Leonetti, to adopt the baby if the Fortunes agreed to pay her for her pain and suffering. Jennifer was still hanging around Emerald Ridge because the Fortunes had held off paying her five hundred thousand dollars to sign over her parental rights because they didn't trust her.

Vivienne wasn't certain whether thinking about Jennifer had conjured her up, but there she was telling the young woman at the reception desk she was there for her facial. A lightbulb went off in Vivienne's head when she whispered to the front-desk supervisor to ask Jennifer if she would like something to drink while she waited to be seen by the masseuse.

Smiling, Jennifer asked, "What do you have?"

"Water, fruit juice, and champagne."

"I'll have the champagne."

Of course, she would choose the champagne, Vivienne thought. Why wouldn't she if she was expecting a half-million-dollar windfall. She waited until Jennifer took several sips, leaving a distinctive lipstick stain on the rim of the glass, then set it on the side table when called for her scheduled facial.

Vivienne scooped up the glass, carefully holding the stem, and went behind the counter to get a plastic bag. Although Jennifer's DNA test had come back as a match for Joey, she still didn't believe it. The woman bore no physical resemblance to the baby. And because she was uneasy about the hospital lab strangely losing the first DNA results to determine the baby's paternity in January, she didn't trust them to handle Jennifer's retest.

She beckoned the supervisor closer. "I'd like to change my appointment to later this afternoon. Could you please check and see if there is an opening?"

The woman tapped several buttons on the computer's keyboard. "I have an opening at four."

Vivienne smiled. "I'll take it."

She felt like a kid in a candy shop when she practically ran in the direction of Poppy's office, hoping her cousin was in. Since fostering Joey, she'd rearranged her schedule, as the director, while relinquishing most the day-to-day responsibility of operating the FGR spa to her manager, Betina Blackfoot.

"Oh, I'm so glad you're here today," she said, breathing heavily as she walked into Poppy's office.

"I only came in because I want to check our inventory." Poppy gave Vivienne an incredulous stare. "Why do you look as if someone's been chasing you?"

Vivienne leaned over and set the plastic bag with the lipstick-stained glass on her cousin's desk. "I believe I might have gotten what we need to prove that Jennifer Johnson isn't Joey's mother."

Poppy combed her fingers through a wealth of long blond hair. "What on earth are you talking about? The results of Jennifer's DNA prove she's Joey's mother."

"If you believe that, then why hasn't she received the half mil she's been asking for?"

"Because not everyone believes she's the baby's mother."

"Exactly." Vivienne's eyes lit up. "And that's why I decided to get an actual sample, and not one she may have forced Joey's birth mother to give her." She told her cousin how Jennifer had been offered a complimentary beverage when she'd come in for her scheduled facial. "We should take it to a private lab to guarantee a fast turnaround and get results we can trust."

Poppy stood up and put the bag with the glass in a large, padded envelope. "I can finish this paperwork another time. I'm ready whenever you are."

Vivienne felt a measure of relief once she and Poppy left the lab a short time later. She had stressed that testing the sample as quickly as possible was crucial and she was willing to pay for a quick turnaround. The receptionist reported that although the lab was swamped because they'd accepted an overflow of tests from the local hospital, she would label it a priority.

She knew she probably would never get another opportunity to get Jennifer's DNA again if it was lost, misplaced, or went missing like *before*.

She'd been in shock when she heard that the DNA from all the Fortune men had mysteriously disappeared from the hospital lab, and they had to retake the test again.

But that wasn't about to happen again. Not on her watch. And once they received the results, then the Fortunes would know for certain if Jennifer was Joey's mother or if she was a scammer.

"Now, we wait," she told Poppy as they headed to the parking lot.

Poppy looped her arm through Vivienne's. "At least we don't have to worry about them losing the sample."

They were feet from the lot when Vivienne saw Annelise Wellington heading in their direction. The three women exchanged warm greetings, Poppy boasting that Annelise's skin-care line, AW GlowCare was selling well at the spa. Vivienne was given samples of Annelise's specially blended moisturizer, body cream, and facial cleanser, and after using them, she'd immediately purchased full bottles.

"I love your skin-care line," she gushed to the pretty brunette, "and I'm not surprised why it's so popular with the clients who visit the spa."

Annelise blushed. "I never could have imagined when I started up a skin-care company less than a year ago that it would take off so well."

"That's because it's an excellent product," Poppy confirmed.

"And I have to thank you for agreeing to carry the samples in your spa," Annelise told Poppy. "Otherwise, I…" She stopped in midsentence as her stepmother approached. "I'm sorry I have to go before I lose my lunch reservation."

Courtney Wellington smiled, and Vivienne curbed the urge to roll her eyes. Courtney always looked as if she was ready for a photoshoot for a glossy fashion magazine. She couldn't wrap her head how widowed Courtney, who hadn't yet celebrated her fortieth birthday, had been married not once or twice, but *three* times.

"Nice seeing you, ladies," Courtney crooned, waving as if she was royalty, then steered Annelise out the parking lot.

"I don't know why, but there's something about that woman that rubs me the wrong way," Vivienne whispered under her breath. "She's so fake."

Poppy nodded. "I agree. However, you must admit she's been a good friend to both our mothers over these past five months, because it's been decades since the Wellingtons and Fortunes have been on friendly terms."

Vivienne wanted to ask her cousin if she'd forgotten Courtney's attempt to work her wiles on Garth once Shelley moved into the Emerald Ridge Hotel following the anonymous text that Garth had fathered Baby Joey. Her excuse of consoling the older man because of the accusation rang hollow to Vivienne. The way she saw it, Courtney was competitive and would do anything within her power to make Wellington Ranch the most prosperous in Emerald Ridge.

"Do you want to hang out and have lunch?" Vivienne asked Poppy.

"I would if I hadn't promised Mom that I would pick up Joey before noon. She has a one-o'clock dental appointment."

Smiling, Vivienne was able to conceal her disappointment. It wasn't often that she was given the chance to drive downtown to shop or indulge in a leisurely lunch or dinner at a few of her favorite restaurants. But she consoled herself with the knowledge that she was scheduled for a massage later that afternoon. And if she was feeling *really* self-indulgent, then she would also book a mani-pedi.

Vivienne walked out of the Emerald Ridge Florist the following day with a bouquet of yellow roses, tulips, and mums. She was excited to join Jonathan for dinner at his house that evening, and because she'd run out of ideas what to bring, she'd decided flowers would be a nice addition to the table. The bouquet would also serve as a peace offering.

She'd informed Drake that she was planning to take a few days off because she'd been working nonstop for weeks and needed a break. He'd given her an I-told-you-so look, then suggested she take more than a few days. He would cover her for a week. She'd quickly accepted his offer because it would give her time to meet with Jonathan to brainstorm how to identify the criminal mastermind.

When she'd told Jonathan she never wanted to speak to him again, Vivienne knew in her heart that she'd lied. And he was the first man whom she could call a friend. Plus, there was Daniel, who'd stirred up emotions she'd never experienced before. She wanted a child of her own someday...and she might have never come to that realization if that adorable little boy hadn't come into her life.

After spending nearly two hours shopping, Vivienne was ready to return to the ranch with her purchases. The storage area in the Volkswagen was nearly filled with shopping bags, and she'd decided to purchase the flowers last to keep from them wilting in the hot car. As she was placing the bouquet on the passenger seat, she heard a woman's voice calling her name, and turned to see Imani and Jonathan pushing their sons in almost identical strollers.

Her eyes met Jonathan's and the wave of heat that began in her chest rushed upward to her face. She prayed he wouldn't notice her blushing like a love-struck adolescent coming face-to-face with the boy which whom she had been crushing. It wasn't only her face that was on fire, but her entire body.

"Hello." Vivienne didn't recognize her own voice.

Jonathan inclined his head. "I didn't expect to run in to you downtown during the middle of day."

"I took some time off to catch up on shopping. How are you, Imani?" Vivienne asked when Colt's mother cleared her throat to get her attention.

"I suppose you and my sister know each other?"

"Of course," she told Jonathan. "I went to visit her at the Fortune Ranch after she'd had Colt." She hunkered down to Colt and Daniel's level, giving each a kiss on the head. "The Fortunes and Porters are family."

Jonathan smiled. "That's something my sister will not let me forget."

Imani took off her sunglasses and perched them on the top of her head. "What I'm *not* going to forget is our stolen family heirloom. And neither is my grandfather. I didn't want to tell him it had been stolen, but unfortunately my mother let the cat out of the bag. Grandpa, who had promised my grandmother he would stop using bad language if she would marry him, broke that promise when he let loose with a stream of curses that would make a drunken sailor blush!" She chuckled softly. "When he finished, my grandmother said she forgave him for cussing because she knows how much that lawn statue means to the family."

Vivienne smiled. She'd met the Porter patriarch and had taken an immediate liking to the man. "If not recovered, lost family heirlooms are impossible to replace."

"That's what I've been telling Jonathan. He told me y'all went to the jail to talk to the prisoner and he kept mentioning ranchers." Vivienne nodded. "Have you given it a thought that maybe it's not one of the big ranchers who paid him, but one or two other smaller ones who got together to cause trouble because they aren't able to compete with the Fortunes or Wellingtons?"

Vivienne stared down at Daniel, who was wiggling and seemingly wanting to get out of the stroller. "That's something I hadn't thought about."

"Neither had I," Jonathan agreed.

"Well, you two need to follow up on my theory. Jonathan, I'm going to take Daniel home with me for a few days while you and Vivienne continue with your investigation."

"You don't have do that," he said.

"Yes, I do," Imani insisted. "After we feed the boys, I want you to put Daniel's car seat in my car—"

"Hold up, Imani," Jonathan interrupted. "You just can't take Daniel with you on the spur of the moment. We didn't plan for this…"

"And we didn't plan for our lawn statue to be stolen. I told you before, I have everything at the ranch I need to care for my *nephew*. Daniel also needs to be around other kids and not stuck with you twenty-four-seven. Besides, he's good for Colt because now he's trying to stand up like his older cousin."

Vivienne, listening to the conversation and witnessing the interaction between Imani and Jonathan, knew that the poor woman had her work cut out for her in convincing Jonathan to let her take his son overnight, or even possibly for several days. She'd witnessed this when he'd left Daniel at day care. Although she didn't want to interfere with what went on between siblings, she knew Imani was right. Daniel needed to spend time with other children closer to his age.

Jonathan's broad shoulders slumped as he took a deep breath. "Fine. You can keep Daniel for a few days."

Imani flashed a triumphant smile. "Thank you! Now, you and Vivienne will have time to put your heads together and try and discover any clues the police may have overlooked."

Vivienne met Jonathan's eyes. "We can begin later today."

"If you're free, then come to my place tonight and we'll go over everything we can recall when talking with Chance."

"Okay."

Imani flashed a Cheshire cat grin. "Thank you, Vivienne. It's good seeing you again, and now Jonathan and I must get out of this heat and feed these two munchkins before they begin acting up."

Vivienne smiled. "Same here. Hopefully when the police catch whoever is behind all the criminal activity, I'll come to Chatelaine and spend some time with you and Nash and the rest of the Fortunes at the ranch."

"That would be awesome! I'm certain everyone will be happy to see you."

Vivienne waved bye-bye to Colt and Daniel, and she was rewarded with Daniel smiling and kicking his legs. She got into her car, started the engine, and switched on the air-conditioning. Sitting and waiting for cool air to flow over her face, Vivienne wondered if she and Jonathan had been able to fool Imani when they'd seemingly arbitrarily set up a date to get together later that evening, when it had already been prearranged. They would have dinner, then discuss what they'd gleaned from Chance that could possibly be enough information to give to the police to identify who could possibly be the person or persons behind the thefts.

Unknowingly, Imani had freed up time for Jonathan, and Drake had done the same for her when he'd volunteered to temporarily fill in as foreman when she got some R&R. Which meant they could spend a lot of time together. It would also allow her to interact with Jonathan the man, and not the single father.

Jonathan stood in the doorway watching the approach of Vivienne's Blue Bayou. He couldn't understand why women tended to give their cars names when it wasn't something most men would do.

Once he'd recovered from Imani hijacking Daniel, he realized she was right about his son being around other children. And it wasn't as if he was handing off Daniel to strangers, just to his sister. Imani told him she wanted to wait at least one day for Daniel to become accustomed to being with her before informing their mother that Daniel was staying over at the Fortune Ranch. She also promised not to allow her nephew to become overwhelmed when confronted with too many people at once.

Jonathan walked over and opened the car door after Vivienne had shut off the engine. Reaching for her hand, he assisted her out, unable to pull his eyes away from her. It was the first time he'd seen so much of her skin exposed. She wore an ice-blue backless sundress ending at her knees with a matching pair of leather ballet flats, while her hair flowed loosely around her face and down her back.

"Wow! You look beautiful."

Vivienne smiled, bringing his gaze to linger on the rose-pink color on her mouth. "I feel beautiful whenever I'm with you."

He was mesmerized by her transformation, wondering if it was going to be possible for him to keep his mind on trying to identify who was responsible for the thefts. If Jonathan had found it challenging to adapt to the role as a new father, it was equally challenging when it came to Vivienne Fortune.

Where he felt he was making progress with Daniel, he was failing miserably with her because what he was beginning to feel for her had him in a quandary. He couldn't deny he was physically attracted to her. After all, she was a gorgeous woman. Beauty aside, it was her patience and gentleness with his son that had him wondering if she would be a good mother to Daniel. However, he had to tread carefully here. His son had lost his birth mom and then been placed with a foster mother. And if he was to have another mother, then he needed one that wouldn't temporarily be in his life. She would have to become his forever mother. And Jonathan wondered if that woman was Vivienne Fortune.

Going on tiptoes, she brushed a light kiss over his mouth. "I brought flowers for the table."

"You went downtown to buy flowers for tonight's dinner?"

"No. I went downtown to do a little shopping now that I'm on what you would call a staycation. Drake has volunteered to run the ranch so I can have time to do things for myself."

"Like shopping?" Jonathan teased.

"That, too. But I was past due for a day of self-care for a facial, massage, and mani-pedi. I usually go shopping and share lunch with my mother once a week and—"

"You shop once a week?" Jonathan asked, cutting her off.

"Only when we want to buy something we need. Do you have a problem with women spending money?"

"No. Not if it's their money."

She arched an eyebrow. "What if it's *your* money, Jonathan?"

"If she were my wife, then no."

"What if she were your girlfriend?

He smiled. "It depends on the girlfriend."

Vivienne returned his smile. "I suppose that makes me a lucky one."

"What are you talking about?"

"Do you recall Chance asking if you were my bodyguard and I told him no, that you were my boyfriend?"

"Sure. But that was just to stop him from insinuating something else."

"You didn't deny I was your girlfriend," she reminded him.

"No, I didn't. Where are you going with this?"

"Where I'm going with this, Jonathan Porter, is if we are going to be seen together when we attempt to ferret out who is behind the criminal activity in Emerald Ridge, then we will have to let folks believe we're involved with each other." She rested a hand over his heart. "And as your girl-friend, I don't need your money, because I have enough to buy whatever I want or need for myself."

Jonathan wanted to tell Vivienne that's why she was different from the other women he'd dated. She didn't need his money. But it wasn't money that would be the deal-breaker. It was Daniel. "I've prepped everything for tonight's menu, so let's go inside and eat."

"I need to get the flowers."

"I'll get them. Are you up to eating outdoors?"

"You don't even have to ask."

Jonathan walked around the car to get the bouquet off the passenger seat, praying he would be able to make it through dinner without letting Vivienne know how much having her in the house without Daniel being present was affecting him.

He'd continued to tell himself that he was just infatuated with her. But who was he kidding? His feelings for her had surpassed liking and now were rapidly bordering on falling in love.

However, it wasn't just about him. He had a child to consider.

Chapter Twelve

"You know we're supposed to be planning strategy on how we plan to uncover the mastermind," Vivienne said as she shifted into a more comfortable position in the hammock next to Jonathan.

He'd made an incredible lobster bisque with pieces of tender lobster meat in a creamy broth, grilled garlicky buttered lobster tails, and an Asian-inspired slaw made with red and green cabbage and shredded carrots with peanut vinaigrette. She'd normally have no more than two glasses of wine with her meal, but had accepted a third glass of rosé to offset the different spices tantalizing her palate.

Jonathan toyed with her hair that was falling over her ear. "You know that's not going to happen tonight, because you're practically falling asleep on me."

She smiled. "That's because the food, drink, the chef, and the ambience all have had a strange effect on me." What appeared to be hundreds of tiny white lights surrounding the patio, outdoor kitchen, and gazebo created a fairy-tale setting that pulled her in to the point that she was loathe to go back indoors.

"That's because we both ate and drank too much, and that means I'm not going to let you drive home by yourself."

"I suppose I can get a rideshare…"

His fingers stilled. "Or the other alternative is you stay over with me, and then drive back to the ranch in the morning."

"If I stay over, then I'm going to need a toothbrush," she informed him.

"You've seen my guest rooms, Vivienne, so you know I always keep a supply on hand. And, just FYI, you're also the first guest to check into this five-star establishment."

"Hmm. What does it offer for it to be rated that high?" she asked playfully.

"Turndown bed service. Gourmet breakfasts served in bed. Egyptian cotton bedding, towels, and bathrobes in different sizes. And the resident chef is willing to prepare whatever a guest requests, providing he has the ingredients in stock."

"Is that so?" she murmured. "Are there any other amenities I should be aware of?"

"Well, there is also a gym if a guest wishes to work out, and a family room where they can view their favorite TV shows and other streaming services. Management is still negotiating with a company to install an in-ground pool. Onsite swimming won't be available until in the fall."

Turning over, Vivienne rested her head on Jonathan's chest, one leg sandwiched between his. "What if I check in for a few days to take advantage of everything you're offering?"

Jonathan met her eyes in the waning daylight. "Are you sure?"

She smiled. "I've never so sure of anything in my life. I'll leave in the morning to pick up several changes of clothes, but I'll be back."

Jonathan knew Vivienne living under his roof for a few days would change their dynamic. His physical attraction to her was obvious and even Imani had called him on it when she'd detected something in his voice whenever he'd said her name. He wasn't certain if his feelings were reciprocated until the night she'd given Daniel a bath. Once she saw him staring at her breasts through her soaked shirt, she'd run out of his house as if a pack of wild dogs were chasing her. It was then she had to know that he'd wanted to sleep with her and had she fled because he was of the belief she hadn't been ready to stay and face what would come next.

"You staying here with me will change everything. Vivienne, we're not kids."

She placed her fingers over his mouth. "You don't have to say anything, Jonathan. We're both consenting adults and I want this. I want *you*. And if we were to sleep together, I don't want to end up with an unplanned pregnancy."

He buried his face in her hair. "Don't worry about that. I have protection." Jonathan smiled when she exhaled a breath. She did not want to be faced with an unplanned pregnancy and neither did he. Once was enough. And if, or when, he did father another child, he wanted it to be with his wife.

"Thank you."

Vivienne had thanked him when he should have been the one thanking her for making it so easy for them to take their friendship to the next level. She was confident, feisty, and outspoken, saying exactly what she wanted without engaging in what he'd thought of as playing head games. He'd thought she was perfect for him, and now she had proven it.

"Let me know when you want to go in?"

"I'm going to hang out here until the sun goes down. I don't have to worry about the bugs because you have a lot of zappers."

Vivienne was right. Once the outdoor kitchen was constructed, he'd purchased several solar-powered bug zappers to ensure comfortable sitting and eating outdoors. "Sounds good. I'll take everything inside, and you can come in whenever you want."

"You can wake me up if I fall asleep. That third glass of wine has me down for the count." Although she'd allowed him to refill her glass, she had only drunk half its contents.

He planted a chaste kiss on her lips. "You're going to have to get off me, sweetheart, so I don't tip the hammock."

Vivienne shifted to where he was able to roll over and get out. Just anticipating what was to come between them had somehow shaken Jonathan's confidence. In the past, he had been the one to determine the terms of his relationship and whether he'd wanted to share his bed with a woman. Somehow, Vivienne had flipped the script; it was *she* who said that not only was she willing to spend the night, but also more than one. And, despite his calm, relaxed demeanor, deep down just anticipating what was to come left him with a newly awakened sense of contentment. It was something that had eluded him before meeting Vivienne.

Jonathan had known with his schedule of flying in and out of the country he hadn't been ready to settle down, but most importantly, not as an absentee father. Phillip Porter had been there for him and Imani until they were in college before he'd finalized the deal to establish Porter Oil in Dubai. During that time, Jonathan was committed to jet-setting until he'd agreed to assist Phillip in Dubai. It had become somewhat of a win-win, because instead of traveling for pleasure, it had become for business.

Now that he was stateside, his life was predictable. He would take care of Daniel, continue to monitor the outpost in Emerald Ridge, and assist Imani once she assumed the position as head of the company's board of directors. It was more responsibility with Daniel becoming the priority. Overseeing Porter Oil and being a full-time father were challenges that he could not afford to fail at.

Jonathan put away all the food, cleaned up the kitchen, and returned outside to find Vivienne sound asleep in the hammock. She had been truthful when admitting the wine had gotten the best of her. He picked her up and carried her into the house. She was snoring lightly when he mounted the staircase and carried her to one of the guest bedrooms. He placed her on the bed, covered her with a lightweight blanket; leaning down he brushed a strand of hair off her cheek, then adjusted the thermostat before he left the room.

Heading downstairs to the family room, he lay across a sofa and thought about the woman sleeping under his roof. Inasmuch as he'd wanted to make love to Vivienne, he knew it wasn't going to happen tonight. She'd promised they would spend several days and nights together, and it was something he was looking forward to.

Vivienne woke, totally disoriented. She was suddenly wide-awake when she realized where she was. She was in Jonathan's house. She recalled relaxing in the hammock after dinner, but not much after that. It was apparent she had fallen asleep, and Jonathan had put her to bed. Never again, she vowed. One or two glasses, but never a third glass. Vivienne wanted to lie there and go back to sleep yet knew if she didn't get out of bed, she would embarrass herself. The pressure on her bladder was increasing with each passing second.

Slipping off the bed, she walked quickly on bare feet to the en suite bath. She relieved herself, then opened a drawer under the twin vanity to find a supply of toothbrushes.

When Jonathan had given her a tour of his home, she'd noticed all the bathrooms were stocked with items available to guests in the finest hotels. Luxury triple-milled French soap, shampoos, rich moisturizers, and a variety of personal-care items filled shelves in a built-in closet. Face, hand, and bath towels and bathrobes in various sizes were also stored in a larger closet. It was obvious Jonathan stocked everything his family or guests needed to enjoy their stay.

Vivienne brushed her teeth, then selected the products she needed to shower and shampoo her hair. Jonathan was right about the amenities available to those he'd invited to come and stay. The spaciousness of his home, the spalike atmosphere of the bathrooms and bedroom suites, with dressing and sitting areas, and the detail of the furnishings in the loggia, outdoor kitchen, and gazebo beckoned her to spend hours there. She took off her dress and underwear, leaving them on a chair, then stepped into shower stall.

She wrapped hair in a thick, absorbent towel, and after drying her body, she slathered on a coconut-scented body cream, and then slipped into a bathrobe. There was just a hint of daylight coming through the blinds of the bedroom windows when she left the bedroom and went downstairs.

Vivienne walked into the kitchen, stopping short when she saw Jonathan sitting at the breakfast island, both elbows resting on the countertop. "Good morning." She removed the towel around her head and tendrils of damp hair fell down her back. Glancing at the clock on the microwave, she saw it was just a few minutes past five.

He smiled. "Good morning to you, too. It looks as if I'm not the only one who gets up with the chickens. I'm forced to get up early because I want to be showered and dressed before Daniel wakes up. What's your excuse?"

Vivienne folded the towel, then sat next to him on the banquette as the scent of soap and clean laundry wafted to her nostrils. He hadn't shaved and the stubble gave him an even more manly aura. "Well, I'm normally an early riser since becoming the ranch's forewoman."

He gave her a sidelong glance. "Do you like being forewoman?"

"I love it."

"How long have you held that position?"

"Five years."

Jonathan lifted strands of her damp hair and brought it to his nose. "You like coconut." It was a statement.

She gave him a direct stare. "Why would you say that?"

"Because you selected coconut when the bathrooms are filled with shampoos and body lotions with a lot of other fragrances."

"I like lavender and coconut. Whenever I take a bath, I use lavender salts because it helps me relax before I fall asleep."

He leaned closer, his nose brushing her ear. "You didn't need it last night when you fell asleep in the hammock."

She blushed. "And I apologize for that. I suppose I'm not a very good guest."

"You stopped being a guest once you slept here."

"But nothing happened, Jonathan," she whispered.

"And it won't until you want something to happen. I've never taken advantage of a woman and I don't want to begin with you. You've become very special to me, and I don't want to do anything to hurt you, or for you to not trust me."

Vivienne wanted to tell Jonathan he was more than special. He was someone with whom she'd fallen in love. "You also are special, Jonathan. And so is Daniel."

Lines fanned out around Jonathan's eyes when he smiled. "So you've come to like the dynamic duo?"

She also smiled. "I love who you call the dynamic duo."

The instant the word *love* slipped out, Vivienne realized it was too late to retract it. She winced. It was too soon to reveal her feelings to Jonathan. Although they had been aware of each other for years, it had only been two weeks since their first personal interaction.

Fortunately, he seemed oblivious to her faux pas when he slipped off the banquette. "I'm going to brew some coffee. Would you like some?"

"Yes, please."

"I know I promised you a gourmet breakfast in bed, so do you want to wait until later, or eat now?"

"I'm only going to stay long enough to have coffee."

His eyebrows lifted. "You know you're welcome to stay as long as you want."

"I know that, Jonathan. But I need to pack a bag with enough clothes to last a few days."

"Pick out an outfit that's a little fancy because I want to take you out tomorrow tonight."

Vivienne slowly blinked. "Are you talking about a date?"

"Yes, Miss Fortune. It's going to be a date. Weren't you the one to say we need folks to think of us as a couple?"

She nodded. "Yes, I did."

"Well, tomorrow night will be the first test. I'm certain the deputy guarding Chance heard you say I was your boyfriend."

"I could've said you were my fiancé."

Jonathan winked at her. "If you were my fiancée, then you would be wearing my engagement ring."

Vivienne did not want to think beyond the ruse they'd concocted to make people believe they were Emerald

Ridge's latest high-profile couple. And if they were instrumental in uncovering clues as to who could be the mastermind, then what was next for them? Jonathan had mentioned he was taking a month off before going back to work to oversee the day-to-day operation of Porter Oil. And, of course, there was Daniel to care for when he did return to the office. Juggling a demanding job and full-time fatherhood wouldn't be easy, and she knew it would leave little time for him to engage in an ongoing association. Even as brief as theirs was predicated to become.

She'd had a few dates over the years that hadn't survived a month, and she didn't expect it would be any different with Jonathan Porter. If she continued to tell herself that, despite her falling in love with Jonathan, perhaps she could prevent him from breaking her heart.

"I'm not your fiancée and I don't have your ring on my finger. Now, where are we going for our first date?"

"Lone Star Selects," he replied. "Unlike your brother Micah, we're not going undercover. We'll act like a normal couple taking in the sights around town. Folks aren't used to seeing me for extended periods whenever I'm in Emerald Ridge and being seen with you will no doubt generate a lot of talk."

"You think someone will ask me about the thefts?"

"Has anyone so far?" Jonathan asked, answering her question with one of his own.

Vivienne shook her head. "I thought it odd that none of the salespeople mentioned it when I was shopping yesterday."

"I'm willing to bet that will change once they see us together."

"Are you saying we're going to give them something to talk about?" she murmured.

"Yes, babe. We're going to give them a *lot* to talk about. And in the end, someone's going to slip up and let the kitty out of the bag about the thefts because there's no such thing as the perfect crime."

"I thought it was letting the cat out of the bag."

"I happen to like kittens," Jonathan said, smiling.

"What do we say when people ask us how long we've been seeing each other?"

"We'll tell them the truth, Vivienne. That we've always liked each other and now that I'm no longer traveling over-seas, we decided to date."

"What about Daniel?" she asked.

"What about him?"

"Do you plan to explain him?"

Jonathan's expression stilled and grew serious. 'He is someone I will *not* explain. Not to anyone. He's my son and my responsibility. And as his father, I will do everything within my power to protect him."

"How long do you plan for us to continue this girlfriend-boyfriend thing?" Vivienne asked.

"It can't be too long. Once Imani brings Daniel back and your staycation ends, it's going to be impossible to hang out together like Miss Marple and Hercule Poirot."

Vivienne's eyes sparkled with excitement. She couldn't believe Jonathan was familiar with one of her favorite au-thors. "You like reading Agatha Christie?"

"I watch the movies based on her books, because I don't have much time to read. And now that I have Daniel, I have even less."

"But what about when traveling? Couldn't you read dur-ing your long flights to pass the time?" she asked.

"I tried it when I first began flying and ended up with

the worst jet lag because I should've been sleeping. I now have a ritual that when I first board, I eat a full meal, drink a lot of water, then go to bed and sleep. I've also learned to never drink anything alcoholic because that also affects jet lag. A flight between here and Dubai takes fifteen hours and I sleep between eight and ten hours before waking up to have a light meal."

Vivienne nodded. "Do you think you're going to miss traveling around the world?"

"I probably would if I didn't have Daniel."

"If we're going to go to Lone Star Selects, I'm certain I can find something suitable for the occasion." She knew the restaurant had a dress code.

"I'm certain you will."

She narrowed her eyes at him. "Why did you say it like that?"

"Like what, Vivienne?"

"Forget it," she countered, wondering if he was alluding to her admitting that she liked to shop. She and Jonathan would only have a short time to act as private investigators attempting to ferret out clues they could give to the police, and she couldn't help hoping that instead of Marple and Poirot, they could become the real-life team of Fortune and Porter.

Chapter Thirteen

Vivienne smiled at Jonathan when he handed her a mug of coffee. She'd found his suggestion they date openly both thrilling and at the same time disappointing because she was aware their so-called open relationship had an expiration date. Her past dating history would have been fodder for gossip if she'd had a relationship of long duration. The only one she could recall that went beyond three months had been with a banker's son from Santa Fe, New Mexico.

They'd shared many things in common, which made her look forward to seeing him again. He would have been, as Darla would say, "the perfect son-in-law," if he hadn't had what Vivienne had come to realize several girlfriends, some who'd had his babies, throughout the Southwest. Once she confronted him, he'd claimed he wasn't a deadbeat dad and he'd financially supported all his children. Vivienne calmly told him it was over between them, and he should buy a house large enough for his baby mamas and children so they all could live as one happy family.

When Micah asked her why she'd ended her relationship with the man and she explained her reason, his comeback was to either do an online search or hire a private investigator to check out her potential future boyfriends. She didn't have to worry about doing a background investigation on

Jonathan Porter though because everyone in Texas was familiar with the Porter name. And despite being a wealthy bachelor, he'd managed to fly under the dating radar in his relationship with Daniel's mother.

Jonathan watched Vivienne intently as she took a sip of the freshly brewed coffee. "Let me know what you think."

Vivienne smiled. "It's perfect."

He picked up his own mug. "This is my first time using a nondairy creamer instead of milk and sugar and I like it."

She took another sip. "Can you substitute the creamer for milk when making cappuccino?

"I'll find out the next time I brew a cup. Do you prefer an American or continental breakfast?"

"Continental during the week and American on weekends." She winked at him. "And I still would like to be your sous-chef."

"I don't need you to be a sous-chef for a continental breakfast, because there's nothing to prep."

"Is it because it's easy like Sunday morning?" she murmured.

"Look at you," Jonathan said, grinning. "You're just full of song titles."

"You don't know the half of it," Vivienne countered. "I have so many songs on my phone's playlist that I listed them on Excel."

"How many do you have?"

"I stopped counting after four hundred," she admitted with a laugh.

"I'd like to synch your phone to my audio system so I can listen to music while I cook."

"Really? Well, I do have an eclectic taste in music genres spanning country, hip-hop, rap, pop, R&B, and soul."

"I like all that."

She smiled. "Thank you."

An awareness popped into his head with the force of a sledgehammer when Jonathan realized how many times Vivienne had sat at his table. They'd connected over two things—Daniel and sharing meals—because that was what families did. How, he wondered, had it happened so quickly, and was it what he wanted and needed at this time in his life?

Daniel was still far too young to ask questions about his mother, and while he was prepared to answer them, Jonathan harbored a fear of alienating his son once he revealed the truth.

Then there was Vivienne. Someone whom he felt was the perfect role model for his son and possibly someone with whom he could plan a future together. They didn't agree on everything, yet it wasn't enough to ruin what they'd developed and that was because they'd come to respect each other's opinions.

Their physical attraction to each other was apparent, although they still hadn't acted on it. Vivienne was confident, mature, and open to their sleeping together, and he knew once they made love, he would not be the same man who'd returned to Emerald Ridge after the phone call telling him he'd fathered a son.

Jonathan had believed after his breakup with Danielle that he would never allow himself to become that vulnerable again. That the woman who'd unknowingly gotten him to fall in love with her had turned his life upside down because she was asking what he'd been able to give her at that time. And once he boarded the jet to fly to Dubai, he'd been able to exorcise Danielle Matthews from his life and his heart once he threw all of his energy into assisting his father growing Porter Oil.

Life had thrown him a curve he'd never expected when

he'd become a father and he now had to come to terms with his ambivalence with the woman sitting across the table from him. He'd likened Vivienne to an itch he couldn't scratch and perhaps that was a good thing, because scratching would either eliminate the itch or make it go away completely. And he didn't *want* her to go away. He wanted to see her, talk to her, and have her play with Daniel and sing to him, and have his son fall asleep in her arms.

Jonathan wanted all these things, then he didn't, because it would only serve to upset the natural order he had established since bringing Daniel home. He recalled what he'd said to Daniel, that it would be just the two of them. They were Team Porter and didn't need anyone else to join them. And what he feared most was Daniel becoming so attached to Vivienne that if or when they broke up, it would emotionally confuse his son, because despite his tender age he'd connected the ringing of the doorbell with Vivienne.

He had to weigh everything before making any decision he made going forward to see how it would affect his son. It was all about Daniel and only Daniel.

Vivienne avoided staring at Jonathan as she drank her coffee because whenever she looked into his large dark eyes, she glimpsed sadness. She didn't know him well, yet there were times when he appeared to tune her out and fall silent. This is when she believed he was still mourning the breakup with Daniel's mother.

"Are you okay?" she questioned.

He smiled, but the gesture was more of a grimace. "Sure. Why?

"It's as if you suddenly zoned out for a moment."

"I was just thinking about a few things," he admitted.

She slid off the banquette. "I'm going to get my things and leave now."

Jonathan's head popped up. "Do you really have to rush off?"

"Yes. I must do a few things at home before I come back." She couldn't tell Jonathan she needed space; a few hours away from him, where she could get her head together and her emotions under control. "I just have to get my bag, then I'm leaving."

Jonathan also stood and stepped toward her, cradling her face in his hands. Lowering his head, he brushed his mouth over hers, deepening the kiss as her lips parted. "I'll see you later, babe. And I'll also call the restaurant to reserve a table for tomorrow night. Don't forget, we should formulate a plan to see if the culprit could possibly be a competing ranch owner."

Vivienne nodded, torn by conflicting emotions. She did not want to leave. Not now. Not when Jonathan's kiss had awakened a passion that sent her pulse racing and her heart thumping madly as she left the kitchen to retrieve her handbag.

Once seated in her vehicle it was a full minute before Vivienne started the engine. It had taken that long for her to feel confident to drive and concentrate on the road, instead of how much Jonathan's kiss had affected her.

She wanted to tell herself it was just a kiss. But, in truth, it wasn't the liplock but rather the man who'd kissed her and under whose roof she'd slept. When she woke to find herself not in Jonathan's bed, but in the guest room, Vivienne knew there was something special about him from the very beginning. While they'd discussed sleeping together, when presented with the opportunity, he hadn't acted on it. He would become the man to which she would measure all others.

Jonathan had reminded her why they were posing as a couple, and it was to identify who was responsible for the thefts and sabotage. For him it was pretend, make-believe. But for her? She so wanted it to be real.

She drove back to the ranch, and when she opened the door to her house, it felt small when compared to Jonathan's. Three thousand square feet was large, but six thousand was twice as large. She loved her home. It was her sanctuary, where she came at the end of the day to unwind and forget about her duties as the ranch's forewoman.

It was where she indulged in leisurely scented baths, binge-watched her favorite series, read for hours until her eyes grew blurry, and where she sat for hours listening to her cell phone's playlist synched with Bluetooth speakers.

Vivienne took off the dress she'd worn the day before, dropped it in a wicker hamper, and slipped into clean underwear, and her ubiquitous white shirt paired with loose-fitting lounging pants. Her cell dinged a familiar ringtone as she walked into the expansive eat-in kitchen.

She activated the speaker feature. "Good morning, Mom."

"How are you?"

"I'm fine."

"Are you?" Darla asked.

"Of course, I am. Why wouldn't I be?"

"I came by your place last night to bring you some hummus I'd picked up from the Grocery, because you raved about it the last time I'd served it. It was late when I dropped by, and I was a little upset because I didn't see your pickup and your house was dark. I told your father that I was going to call Drake to check on you and he told me to let it go."

"Dad's right," Vivienne replied. "I had dinner with Jonathan Porter and ended up drinking too much wine. I didn't want to drive home buzzed, so I wound up spending the night."

There was a distinct pause before Darla said, "Is what you have going on with Jonathan serious?"

"How serious are you alluding to?"

"You know what I mean, Vivienne."

"No, I don't know, Mom. If you want to ask if we are sleeping together, then the answer is no. I slept in one of his guest bedrooms." There was another moment of silence from the other end. "What, Mom? No comeback? I know you want to see me with someone you claim will make me happy. What you don't understand is that I am happy with my life. Right now, Jonathan is a wonderful friend I like spending time with. If we do happen to sleep together that doesn't necessarily translate into you becoming mother of the bride. One Fortune wedding this year is enough."

"Don't you see yourself getting married sometime in the future?" Clearly her words had fallen on deaf ears and Darla was digging in her heels.

"I would like to be married one of these days even though it isn't at the top my wish list." Vivienne huffed out a breath. "You know I'm cautious with men because I haven't had the best track record in the romance department."

"Because you love with your heart and not with your head. You must learn to combine the two. When I first met your father, I knew he had everything I was looking for in a man. Once I realized I could not imagine my life without him, I knew I had fallen in love with him."

Vivienne wanted to tell her mother she could not look that far ahead. Yes, she was falling in love with Jonathan and because she feared she was in too deep, she had made it a concerted effort to dial back her emotions.

"Jonathan and I are *not* getting married."

"If you say so."

"I say so, Mother. We're going to meet later this afternoon to plan strategy how we can identify the person or
persons who'd orchestrated the thefts and sabotage."

"Shouldn't you leave that for the police?" There was a
note of concern in Darla's voice.

"It wasn't the police, but Micah who was able to apprehend the thief. This is not to say that Jonathan and I can't
come up with some evidence that will help the police crack
the case."

"I just want you to be careful," Darla said.

"Don't worry, Mom. I'm certain we won't do anything
that would interfere with the police's investigation."

"Drake told me that he's filling in for you for a few days.
Do you think we could schedule a day when we can have
lunch at either Francesca's or the Emerald Ridge Café? I'm
up for either one."

Vivienne smiled. "Of course. I really like Francesca's."

"Then Francesca's it is. You can call me and let know
what's good for you."

"Okay, I will."

She ended the call and tapped the music app, smiling
when Shania Twain singing "When You Kiss Me" floated
from the speaker. Sinking down to a chair, Vivienne closed
her eyes and listened to the lyrics, when she recalled the
tenderness when Jonathan had cradled her face and kissed
her. In that instant, she knew she couldn't keep lying to
herself. She had fallen so unescapably in love with a man,
and when he had kissed her, it had ignited a fiery passion
in her that left her more frightened than any other time in
her life. Frightened because she feared she would not become a part of his future.

Once she'd ended a relationship, it as if she'd mentally erased the man from her memory. She had to ask herself if it would be as easy with Jonathan and the answer was no. She wouldn't be able to forget him or Daniel. The little boy had stolen her heart. The song ended and she got up to gather the ingredients she needed to prepare breakfast. Then she had to go through her closets to select what she needed to pack to take to Jonathan's house.

Jonathan relaxed in a lounge chair on the loggia, waiting for the cleaning service employees to complete their tasks. He'd contracted with the company to come twice a month to clean the house. There wasn't much they had to do with him being out of the country so often. It was different now because he planned to live there every day for the next five or even six years. Daniel had made the house a home. His little boy had made them a *family*.

He was trying not to think of Vivienne being part of that equation, although she was so good for his son, and Daniel seemed to adore her. It could be she'd taken the place of his foster mother, who had taken such good care of him.

Jonathan knew Daniel wasn't the only Porter male who'd fallen under Vivienne Fortune's spell. Everything about her appealed to him and he'd concluded that she was perfect. She'd checked off all the boxes, yet something wouldn't allow him to tell her how much she'd come to mean to him.

Suddenly it hit him like a sledgehammer breaking down a door. He was doing it again. He was setting up a test to measure a woman's worth. This time, it wasn't about money but whether she would be a good mother for his son. His idea that they pose as a couple to see if they could uncover the person or persons behind the thefts was merely a smokescreen. That wasn't something they should be doing as victims of a crime.

It had been too long since he'd dated a woman and he'd missed spending several hours in an eating establishment, being served while laughing and chatting about things he deemed inane. It was intimate dining that he had come to enjoy most when interacting with a woman, and Jonathan prayed he wasn't reverting to old habits when it came to women. That he'd had an ulterior motive when he just should've accepted who they were. After all, how could he expect perfection when he was so flawed?

Jonathan didn't want to hurt Vivienne. He cared too much for her. He shook his head. Even that was a lie. His feelings for her went far beyond caring. What frightened him was that he was falling in love with her. There wasn't anything about her he did not love; however, it couldn't be all about himself. Now, there was Daniel. It was difficult and challenging learning to be a father and he didn't want to complicate things by becoming emotionally involved with a woman. If they were able to sleep together and continue without declarations of love, then it would isolate him from heartbreak.

His cell phone dinged a text message. Reaching over, he picked it off a side table. Vivienne was on her way.

"Do you mind if I clean up the kitchen?" Vivienne asked Jonathan, placing her napkin on the table. Over dinner, they'd discussed driving over to the ranches not affected by the thefts, then realized because they weren't detectives, it was unlikely they would find any stolen horses out in the open. Scrapping their plans had made her more frustrated than ever.

She was surprised when he nodded. It was the first time

he'd allowed her to clear the table, because aside from her helping Jonathan prepare a meal, he'd jealously guarded his kitchen like a hen protecting her chicks.

Vivienne smiled when one of her favorite tunes came through the speakers Jonathan had installed throughout the first floor. She began singing along with Dierks Bentley's "Come a Little Closer." She was scraping dishes and stacking them in the dishwasher when she felt movement behind her. She looked up to find Jonathan approaching her. One second, she was standing, then without warning he'd swept her up off her feet, as she held on to his neck to keep her balance.

There was no need for talk. The song's lyrics said it all, she realized, when she buried her face against the column of Jonathan's neck and pressed a kiss under his ear. The silent storm that had been brewing when she'd stood in his kitchen watching him brew cappuccino for her suddenly erupted in a maelstrom of passion, short-circuiting every nerve in her body.

You staying here with me will change everything.

Jonathan was right. Her agreeing to spend the night in his house would change her. After making love, they would never be the same people they were before.

Closing her eyes, Vivienne allowed her senses to take over as she breathed in his clean masculine scent, pressed her mouth against the steady beating pulse under his ear, and reveled in his powerful arms carrying her effortlessly up the staircase. Her eyes were still closed as he placed her on the bed, his body following hers down. She felt his hands brush her breasts, and then slowly unbutton her blouse. She heard his intake of breath, then opened her eyes to find him staring at her breasts in her sheer bra. It seemed like an eternity before he removed each article of her clothing until she lay completely naked.

She became a voyeur, watching him undress, removing his shirt, jeans, and boxer briefs, then tossing them in a pile at the foot of the king-sized bed. He was a deeply bronzed god come to life with his lean, muscled body; just gazing at him had heated her blood to where she felt it was boiling. The side of the mattress dipped slightly as he slid in beside her, his hand going under the pillow to retrieve a condom. Vivienne was certain he heard her expel a sigh of relief. Now that she was resigned to becoming a mother, she wanted to plan for a baby, and she didn't want history to repeat itself with Jonathan if they were to experience an unplanned pregnancy. He quickly opened the packet and slipped on the latex sheath.

Jonathan gave her breasts his undivided attention as waves of pleasure raced through her, and just when she felt as if she was about to climax, he entered her until they'd become one with the other. Vivienne gloried in the hard body atop hers. Shivers of delight took her higher as moans slipped past her lips. She lost track of time until she was forced to let go as her first orgasm took over, holding her captive for mere seconds before another earth-shattering release rocked through her core. Taking her beyond to where she'd never been as Jonathan groaned out his own release, breathing the last of his passion into her mouth.

"You are so incredibly beautiful," Jonathan whispered in Vivienne's ear as her body calmed from release. What he'd wanted to tell her was that he loved her passion, her femininity, and her strength. He loved how she related to Daniel and his son to her.

"It's because you make me feel beautiful," Vivienne whispered.

He was beginning to love everything about Vivienne Fortune, but feared having to depend on her emotionally. He went to bed thinking of her. Woke thinking of her. The moment she walked into his home it brightened like a ray of sunshine, and when she left, he found himself waiting for her return. He'd begun to feel like a hamster on a wheel, going around and around with his emotions and not being able to stop.

Jonathan knew he had to stop seeing Vivienne so often because of his increasing dependency on her. He was losing focus when he had to learn how to be a good dad and not complicate things by falling for a woman. It had become even more complicated now that they'd slept together.

"Don't move. I'll be right back."

Vivienne moaned softly. "Don't take too long."

He went into the bathroom to discard the condom and, standing at the vanity, he stared at his image in the mirror. It wasn't that he'd changed physically. What he'd recognized was fear and indecision. It was what he'd experienced when answering the phone and hearing that he'd fathered a child. His first impulse was to laugh it off, but being responsible for creating another human being was as serious as it could get.

Jonathan returned to the bedroom and got into bed with Vivienne. Her face was still flushed from their lovemaking and her hair flowing over the pillow was as sensual as the woman who unknowingly had crept under the barrier he'd erected to keep women at a distance.

He buried his face in her hair, as panic like he'd never known before welled inside him. It wasn't that he'd found himself wanting Vivienne Fortune. He also needed her.

Chapter Fourteen

Jonathan had kept his promise to Vivienne when he served her breakfast in bed after they managed to get about four hours of uninterrupted sleep after making endless love. It was if both had become insatiable and agreed to stop before they wouldn't be able to get out of bed in the morning.

He set his bed tray on the bedside table when his phone vibrated. Reaching over, he peered at the screen. It was Imani. "I have to take this," he told Vivienne when she looked at him. "Stay," he said, holding on to her arm as she attempted to get out of bed. "Good morning, Imani. Is Daniel giving you trouble?"

"Of course not. He's such a good baby. I'm calling because I'm bringing him back. Unfortunately, we had a slight misunderstanding with a vendor at the boutique and Nia needs help straightening it out."

Jonathan sat up straight. "You don't have to bring him back. I'll come and get him."

"That's okay. I don't mind bringing him to you."

"Are you sure, Imani?"

"Of course, I'm sure."

"Thanks." It was the last thing he said to his sister before hanging up.

"Is Daniel okay?" Vivienne asked, her blue eyes filled with concern.

"Yes. My sister must take care of a work crisis and she's bringing Daniel back home." Vivienne set her tray on the table on her side of the bed. "Where are you going? You haven't finished eating your eggs Benedict."

"I'm leaving, Jonathan. Your sister doesn't need to know that I'm sleeping with her brother."

"Don't be silly, Vivienne."

"I'm not being silly! It's just that I don't like advertising who I sleep with. Being seen in public with you is one thing, but there's no need for your sister to see us hugged up together."

"Don't you mean *shacked up*?"

Vivienne rolled her eyes at him. "I said exactly what I meant."

Jonathan didn't want to argue with her. Not after the passion they'd just shared together. "Okay. I'll have to cancel tonight's dinner reservation because I don't have a baby-sitter."

Vivienne smiled at him over her shoulder. "Don't worry, Jonathan. There may come a time in the future when we can have a date night."

He watched her as she slipped out of bed and walked into the bathroom. He waited, then gathered both trays and went downstairs to clean up before Imani arrived.

Jonathan paced the floor holding Daniel, who wouldn't stop crying. He'd tried giving him his pacifier, but he just spat it out. He'd begun to cry when Imani walked out of the house, his little arms reaching for his aunt.

"It's okay, buddy. Your auntie Imani had to do something, and she couldn't take you with her."

Just when he'd felt he was making progress in learning to be a father, he now felt wholly inadequate because he couldn't calm his son. Imani told him she'd fed Daniel breakfast and that meant he wasn't hungry.

At that moment, Jonathan realized he needed Vivienne more than ever. He wanted to call and ask her to come and help him with his baby, but that would be akin to using her. And that was something he refused to do. Daniel cried until exhausted, his little body jerking as he continued to whimper. Jonathan continued to walk and gently rock him until he finally fell asleep. Rather than place him in his crib, he sat on the glider and cradled him against his chest.

It didn't take the intelligence quotient of a rocket scientist to know Daniel gravitated to women. Firstly, there had been Danielle, then his foster mother, Vivienne, and now Imani. There had to be something about their voices that had had a calming effect on him. Daniel needed to be comforted. And while Jonathan was beginning to trust people again, the fact that he needed a woman was still unsettling.

He'd thought about hiring the town matchmaker, Naomi Katz, to try and find him a wife. He knew it would end up being a strictly business arrangement, because he still wasn't ready to open his heart to anyone other than his son. Jonathan quickly dismissed the idea. Whoever he selected to share his life would have to love his son unconditionally.

Daniel woke up and began screeching again, forcing Jonathan to swallow his machismo to call Vivienne.

Fortunately, she picked up on the first ring and came right over upon receiving his SOS.

Vivienne glared at Jonathan as she held Daniel, who was resting his head against her breasts. When she'd walked into the house, it was to Daniel's hysterical crying. "What on earth did you do to him?"

"Nothing. He started crying when Imani dropped him off because he didn't want her to leave."

"It had to be more than that, Jonathan Porter."

"I'm telling you it wasn't, Vivienne Fortune."

"I'll stay until it's time for you to put Daniel down for the night."

"You don't have to leave. The invitation is still open for you to stay over."

Vivienne thought about sleeping in the house with Jonathan and Daniel. She didn't know why, but it made her slightly uncomfortable. It was as if they were playing house. "No, Jonathan."

"Please, Vivienne."

She met Jonathan's eyes. He hadn't asked her to stay. He'd pleaded with her, and it was the first time he'd exhibited a modicum of vulnerability. As a new father, he'd always appeared confident and in control. It was as if he had an innate ability to know exactly what to do with Daniel.

"Okay. I'll stay. But only for tonight."

Jonathan clasped his hands together in a prayerful gesture. "Thank you."

She nodded. "You're welcome."

Vivienne's one night became two, then three, and several more, allowing her a glimpse of what her life would be if she and Jonathan were married. They'd shared a bed, meals, and Daniel, until it came time her to return to the ranch and resume her duties as the forewoman.

Drake smiled at her when she entered his office. "How was your staycation?"

She flopped down on the sagging sofa cushions. "It was nice."

"Did you get a chance to relax?"

"Yes. Why are you asking?"

"Because," her brother began, running a forefinger under his eye, "even though you managed to get some sun on your face, it isn't enough to conceal the dark circles under your eyes. What's the matter? Porter keep you up all night?" he teased, grinning.

Vivienne's jaw dropped, heat suffusing her face, and seconds later, she asked, "What are you talking about?"

"Come now, Vivienne. Even though you've tried to keep it on the down-low, I know that you've been seeing Jonathan Porter."

"I'm not seeing him on what you call *the down-low*. That sounds so sleazy."

"My bad. Maybe I should've said like they used to say back in the day that that you are courting or keeping company."

"It was neither. I was simply helping Jonathan with his son."

"Mom told me his son's mother passed away."

"Yes."

"That can't be easy for him. I can't imagine becoming a father at this time in my life, or even worse, a single father."

"You don't want children?" Vivienne asked curiously.

"I'm not saying that. It's just I'm not ready for them."

Vivienne stared down at the drying mud on the toes of her boots. "There was a time when I'd told myself that I didn't want children either."

"What changed?" Drake asked.

"Daniel Porter."

"Is it Daniel or Daniel's father?"

"It's both, Drake. I respect Jonathan because he is totally devoted to his son and has given up international travel until Daniel is old enough to be enrolled in school. He says he'll take his boy overseas with him during school recess and summer vacations."

"That's because once you become a parent you must be willing to sacrifice a lifestyle that's not conducive to raising kids."

Vivienne wanted to remind Drake that she wasn't and had never been a party girl, and there wasn't that much for her to sacrifice. Bracing her hand on the sagging cushion, she pushed to her feet. "I'm going over to check on the workers putting the new roof on the breeding barn. Word of caution, dear brother. If you don't replace this sofa, I'm going to purchase one and tell Micah to take it out of your paycheck. Every time I sit on it, I must go to the spa for a massage."

"Not to worry, dear sister. I ordered a new sofa, and I expect it to be delivered in a couple of weeks. Oh, I forgot to tell you that Mom wants us to come to the house around seven for what she's calling a little repast. She's complaining that she doesn't see her kids enough."

"She does see us, Drake, because we all live on the same ranch," she reminded him.

"I think she's talking about all of us sitting down to dinner together."

Vivienne knew Darla Fortune missed sharing meals with her children once all of them had moved into their own homes on the ranch.

"If you see Mom, then tell her I'm coming."

Vivienne thought about her conversation with Drake about Jonathan as she went about her duties at the ranch. She hadn't lied to her brother when she'd admitted staying over at Jonathan's house to help him take care of Daniel and that she'd enjoyed what she'd termed "playing house." Jonathan was the daddy, she the mommy, and Daniel their son. She and Jonathan shared a bed, while Daniel slept across the hall in his crib. They made love and showered together, laughing and splashing each other like kids. Jonathan cooked, while she fed Daniel; the baby's naptime was when they huddled together in the hammock, or retreated to the family room to read or watch television. Her agreement to stay one night had turned into a week and her impromptu staycation ended much too soon for her once she had to return to the ranch.

Vivienne stood a short distance away from the breeding barn and smiled. Rays of brilliant sun reflected off the new, dark green, all-weather roof that had replaced the leaky one. She went inside and stopped at a stall of a springing heifer in the breeding barn, watching movement in the heifer's protruding middle. Reaching over, she rubbed the animal's neck. "I know you're uncomfortable, but the vet says you'll have your baby any day now." The cow turned her head, looked at her, and let out a low mooing. "You're going to have a beautiful, healthy calf, just like the last time." Just then, her phone rang, and Vivienne took it from the back pocket of her jeans. "What's up, Poppy?"

"Where are you?"

"I'm at the ranch. Why?"

"I must tell you something in person. I'm at the spa now and as soon as I hang up, I'll meet you at your house."

Vivienne looked at her phone when her cousin abruptly ended the call, completely puzzled as to what Poppy wanted to talk about. She left the barn, got into her truck, and drove home. She was opening the door when Poppy pulled up and got out of her vehicle.

She looped her arm through her cousin's. "What's so important that you couldn't tell me on the phone?"

Poppy's brilliant green eyes flashed with excitement. "I got the results back from the private lab and they verify that Jennifer Johnson is *not* Baby Joey's mother."

Vivienne screamed, then clapped a hand over her mouth. "Oh my gosh!"

"I confronted Jennifer, asking how she got her hands on the real mother's DNA."

"And what did she say?"

"She claims she's not going to say a damn word unless she's paid five hundred thousand dollars."

Vivienne shook her head. "Oh, hell no! Does she really believe she can con the Fortunes out of that kind of money?"

"She probably believes she can. What I plan to do is string her along and hopefully I'll be able to catch her with the real mother, who probably is behind the con."

"What I don't understand, is why would the birth mom hire someone to be her? And was she the one who'd attempted to kidnap Joey two months ago because she changed her mind?"

"I don't know, Vivienne, but I'm not going to stop until I find out who's behind this scam."

She shook her head in disbelief. "I can't believe the Fortunes have become the targets of criminal activity. Firstly, someone is attempting to extort a half million dollars by selling a newborn, and then there are the thefts and sabotage targeting our ranch and a few large ranches, not to mention the theft of Jonathan Porter's priceless family heirloom lawn statue. It's as if the criminals are having a field day running amok in Emerald Ridge."

"When you say priceless…how much is that statue worth?"

A beat passed, then Vivienne said, "The appraisal is in the same ballpark as what Jennifer Johnson is asking."

With wide eyes, Poppy said, "You're kidding?"

Vivienne shook her head. "I wish I was."

"It's got to stop and the people responsible have to be caught, charged, and incarcerated."

"It's going to happen," Vivienne said optimistically. "Someone will let it slip about what they know or overheard and it's like an analogy to a falling row of dominoes. Touch one and all the others follow."

"Let's hope you're right," her cousin said. "If you hadn't thought of getting Jennifer's DNA without her knowledge, we would've continued to believe that she's Joey's mother. And now that she knows we're on to her, she has two options. Hang around until we uncover the real mother, or if she's smart, she will leave Emerald Ridge ASAP."

"Something tells me she's not going anywhere until she's paid."

"If that's the case, I'm going to stick closer to her than fleas on a dog's back." Poppy hugged Vivienne. "Gotta run back to the spa because it's Betina's day off." The FGR spa manager, Betina Blackfoot, had assumed the day-to-day operation of the spa once Poppy was given approval to foster Baby Joey.

Jennifer Johnson is not Baby Joey's mother. Even hours later, when she'd showered and changed into a dress for dinner with her family, Poppy's statement continued to play over and over in Vivienne's head like the incessant buzzing from a nest of disturbed hornets.

She parked her Volkswagen next to Drake's Porsche at the rear of the wing of the mansion belonging to her parents.

Her brothers teased her mercilessly when she'd purchased the small car, yet admitted to giving her a pass because it was a convertible. Blue Bayou was the perfect alternative to the Ram 1500 she drove working on the ranch.

Vivienne entered the house through a rear door, then followed the sounds of voices until she found everyone in the smaller dining room. Darla only used the formal dining room when hosting large gatherings of ten or more. Smiling, she approached her new sister-in-law and embraced her.

"Have you gotten used to being a married woman?" she asked Jacinta.

The beautiful petite woman with dark brown hair and light brown eyes blushed. "Not yet," she whispered. "I still can't believe how much I've come to love Micah."

"And my brother is madly in love with you." What had begun as a marriage of convenience turned into one where both had fallen inexorably in love with each other.

"I can't thank you enough for all you did to help make our wedding day not only special, but also spectacular."

Once Micah announced he was marrying Jacinta Gomez, Vivienne volunteered to assist her when she'd hired a much sought-after wedding planner to hold the wedding on the ranch, rather than at a town hall, which had been Jacinta's choice to have the ceremony.

Vivienne smiled. "You could say I did it because I wanted a sister."

Jacinta's eyelids fluttered. "And you are my sister in every sense of the word."

Vivienne walked over to the buffet server lined with trays of hot and cold food. She bumped Drake's shoulder. "So much for a light repast," she whispered.

Picking up a plate, he handed it to her, then took one for

himself. "When I mentioned it to Mom, she said she ordered enough so whatever is left over we can take home."

"Nice." Darla had ordered a charcuterie platter of meats, cheese, olives, fruits, crackers, and nuts. Hors d'oeuvres included ginger hoisin chicken drumettes, honey sesame glazed cocktail sausages, skewered shrimp, bacon-wrapped scallops, deviled eggs, mini deviled crab cakes, and dill pancakes with salmon caviar, and lemon crème fraiche. There were also a variety of dipping sauces and bowls of chilled salads.

Hayden entered the room, smiling. "It's nice to see that everyone got the memo. Now, let's see what everyone is eating. What the..." He swallowed a curse when he saw what his wife had selected for dinner. "I thought we were having barbecue."

Darla rested a manicured hand on her husband's shoulder. "I decided to change it up a bit. We're only weeks away from July Fourth and I promise we'll go all out with barbecue."

Hayden dipped his head and kissed his wife. "Thank you, my love."

"Y'all need to get a room," Micah said, laughing.

"We have rooms, and plenty of them since you knuckleheads moved out." Hayden smiled at Vivienne. "Of course, baby girl, you're not included in the knucklehead category."

Vivienne executed a graceful curtsey. "Thanks, Dad."

Her mother mentioning July Fourth meant the end of the month was fast approaching and still no one had uncovered who had masterminded the mayhem at several ranches. And despite scientific proof that Jennifer Johnson wasn't Baby Joey's biological mother, his real parents were still out there somewhere. Plus, Daniel would celebrate his first birthday before the end of the month and Jonathan's paternity leave would also come to an end.

Speaking of which… Jonathan had asked her about childcare for Daniel, and she'd had him fill out an application for his son to be enrolled at the Fortune's Gold Ranch day care whenever there was an opening. The day care had been set up for employees and guests with a small staff of experienced sitters. The end of the month would also signal a drastic shift in their relationship. Jonathan would have to divide his time working for Porter Oil and focus on caring for Daniel.

Jonathan wasn't just a single father, but he was a hands-on father. A baby he'd claimed he'd known nothing about until the beginning of the month had become his whole world. What he hadn't known was she wanted to become a part of his world.

Vivienne filled her plate from with items from the charcuterie platter, then picked up a smaller plate and helped herself to some Greek salad. Balancing a plate in each hand, she walked over to the table, then sat next to Jacinta. She speared a dolma, took a bite, and slowly chewed the delicious grape leaf filled with a mixture of rice, spices, dried currants, and pinenuts.

Vivienne noticed, when sharing meals with Jonathan, that he, too, tended to follow a Mediterranean diet, with a lot of fruit, whole grains, vegetables, beans, nuts, and healthy fats. She'd overeaten when he'd served grilled, garlic-herb rack of lamb with couscous and a Greek salad. Not only would she miss seeing Jonathan so often, but she would also miss his cooking for her.

"Vivienne, your father is talking to you."

She jumped slightly when Jacinta nudged her. Vivienne

hadn't realized she'd zoned out when thinking about Jonathan. "Yes, Dad?"

"I was asking if it's true about you and Porter teaming up to find out who's behind sabotaging the ranchers?"

"It was."

Hayden lifted bushy, sandy eyebrows. *"Was?"*

Reaching for the napkin beside her plate, Vivienne touched it to the corners of her mouth. "Yes. Once we left the jail after talking to the convicted thief, we couldn't ignore his reference to ranchers competing with one another. And that got us to thinking maybe it could be some of the smaller ranchers who hadn't been targeted. That they resented being eclipsed by large ranches like ours and the Wellingtons." She sampled a shrimp and swallowed before continuing. "We'd thought about driving over to the Double C or Hampton Verde to see if we could find some of the stolen horses, then scrapped that plan and decided to let the police do what they're paid to do. It would've leveled a lot of suspicion on the Fortunes if someone had spotted me on their property."

Hayden raised his glass of sweet tea. "I'm glad you decided to end your amateur sleuthing and leave the investigations to men licensed and paid to carry firearms."

Vivienne couldn't believe what had come out of her father's mouth. It was apparent Hayden's machismo was on full display, and watching her mother's expression it was obvious she wasn't too pleased with her husband's pronouncement.

"I love watching movies with female sleuths," Darla said. "My favorite is *Miss Fisher's Murder Mysteries*. Phryne Fisher wears wonderful clothes, carries a pearl-handled pistol, and toys with Inspector Jack Robinson's affections, where he doesn't know whether he's coming or going. And that makes her an independent woman who doesn't need or want a man to control her life."

"I'm hooked on *Frankie Drake Mysteries*," Jacinta said, smiling, "because of the four diverse lead female characters, two who run a detective agency in nineteen-twenties Toronto, Canada. And Frankie is my kind of woman because she was liberated decades before the women's liberation movement in this country in the nineteen-sixties."

"Whoa, Nellie! How in the giddy up did we go from talking about ranch thefts and sabotage to television shows with made-up women detectives?" Hayden asked.

"You were the one who mentioned sleuthing," Darla reminded him. "We just said our favorite female sleuths could've been based on real-life people. You probably wouldn't be so fired up if we'd mentioned Hercule Poirot, Sherlock Holmes, or even Edgar Allan Poe's C. Auguste Dupin."

"You tell him, Mom," Vivienne quipped.

Hayden glared at his sons. "Are any of you going to have my back?"

Micah shook his head. "Nope."

"You started it, Dad, so you're on your own, Drake added.

Vivienne knew her father had been bested when he got up from the table to refill his plate. It was only when Hayden Fortune knew he was on the losing side of a conversation that he would finally toss in the towel. Especially with his wife, to whom he'd been married for thirty-seven years. Underneath Darla's kind and loving exterior was a woman who knew what she wanted and wasn't afraid to go after it. The characteristic was something Vivienne had learned from her mother when she'd decided she wanted to be the forewoman for the ranch.

The focus of the conversation segued from Emerald Ridge's criminal activity to the announcement of a recipient to be awarded a Gift of Fortune invitation. Vivienne and Drake revealed the contents of the nominations to everyone and would have to decide on the winner in less than a week.

Vivienne returned to her home after spending more than two hours with her family, armed with several bags filled with leftovers that Darla had packed up for her. There was enough to last her for several days, and that meant she didn't have to cook. After storing the containers in the fridge, she decided to turn in for the night, aware there would be many more nights to come where she would sleep alone. It had been four days since she'd last shared a bed with Jonathan, but it felt like forty. Somehow, she'd come to depend on him not only physically, but also emotionally. And it was the latter that frightened her most, because she would not, and *could not*, allow herself to become that vulnerable.

She equated vulnerability to heartache—and as a Fortune, it was an emotion they'd struggled with. She witnessed what it had done to Micah before he met, fell in love with, and married Jacinta. She'd been there for Poppy when she'd gone through a divorce. As well as Rafe, who'd lost his wife and toddler son in a car crash, and Shane, who was a divorced father of a six-year-old son.

Now, with her heart on the line, she prayed not to become the next Fortune to experience what it would feel like to have it broken.

Chapter Fifteen

Vivienne had gotten an e-vite from Jonathan for Daniel's first birthday party, and after accepting it took an entire day for her to decide what to buy for a one-year-old whose father had the resources to give him whatever he wanted or needed.

She'd driven to the baby store, searching aisles upon aisles of age-appropriate toys, and then it suddenly hit her that Daniel didn't need toys as much as he would books. Her mother had instilled a love of reading at an early age and Vivienne had learned to read at five, a full year before she was enrolled in school. She went online and ordered the delivery of a boxed set of twelve iconic Little Golden Books, the titles listing all her childhood favorites, and another book with thirty, five-minute, easy-to-read adventures.

Happy with her purchase, Vivienne covered the books with colorful birthday wrapping paper and put them in a decorative shopping bag.

Jonathan sat Daniel on his lap in front of the computer monitor as the images of his mother, aunts, and grandparents in a prearranged video party Imani had set up the day before filled the screen. They were in New Orleans where they were scheduled to take a week-long vacation. Imani had called to say she wouldn't be able to attend the birthday party in person because Colt had come down with a cold and she didn't want Daniel to catch it.

"You have to stop trying to take off your party hat," Jonathan said to Daniel as his family sang the birthday song. All too soon, the video party ended and he sent Vivienne a text message that she was welcome to come over for ice cream and cake at whatever time was convenient for her.

Daniel had practically destroyed the paper hat when Jonathan removed the elastic tie under his chin. "You're going to have to get used to wearing a hat, buddy, because as a Texan we wear Stetsons. Daddy will help you learn the rules about wearing and removing your hat, so you won't embarrass yourself. Okay?"

Jonathan powered down the desktop and carried Daniel into the kitchen for his dinner of mac and cheese, fruit, and milk. The birthday boy fed himself cubes of watermelon with his hands, then grasped the sippy cup, drank, and expelled a loud burp. The sound had startled him until he began laughing and burped again, while Jonathan slowly shook his head. Instead of telling Daniel that it wasn't polite to deliberately burp, he decided to ignore it. Whenever he'd attempted to chastise his son for inappropriate behavior, it was if he'd given the child the go-ahead to do it again.

Daniel finished his dinner and Jonathan was wiping his face and hands with a damp facecloth when the doorbell rang. The baby went still, then began wiggling to free himself as Jonathan tightened his hold around his body. Then Daniel let out an ear-piercing scream that nearly deafened Jonathan. Wincing from the sound, he tapped the app on his phone connected to the doorbell camera and saw Vivienne.

Moments later, he opened the door and Daniel practically jumped out of arms and into Vivienne's. She caught him with one arm while struggling to hold on to her shopping bag.

"Can you take the bag?" she asked Jonathan who was as excited to see her as his son.

Once he complied, Vivienne cradled Daniel to her chest. Jonathan's chest expanded as he watched his son pat her face with both hands, then leaned in to plant a wet kiss on her cheek. "Thank you for the kiss." She waltzed around the great room, singing the birthday song as Daniel joined her in a language known only to him.

It was nearly a week since she'd last held him and he could tell that now Vivienne didn't want to let him go.

"Have you heard back about the application for Daniel's day care?" Jonathan asked.

"Not yet. I'll make certain to follow up and get back to you."

"Thank you. Daniel just ate dinner, so if it's okay with you, I'd like to wait a while before we have ice cream and cake."

"That's fine with me. No hurry. I'm free for the rest of the night." Her response elicited a smile from Jonathan. From the sound of it, Vivienne was looking just as forward to spending time with him and Daniel as they were with her.

"Come with me and I'll show you the party room."

Vivienne followed Jonathan into the kitchen, laughing when she saw helium-filled happy birthday balloons tied to chairbacks with colorful ribbons. "Whose idea was this?"

"Imani's. She would've come if Colt didn't come down with a cold."

A look of compassion filled her lovely face. "There's nothing worse than sick baby because they can't tell you what's wrong."

"Or a crying one when he isn't sick."

Jonathan was referring to when he was forced to call her to come to his home because Daniel wouldn't stop crying. He was grateful that she'd been there for him during his time of need.

"Adults want babies to talk, then when they learn and repeat everything, they hear it becomes a problem," she murmured.

"You've got that right."

Vivienne set Daniel on the floor, and he crawled over to a chair and pulled himself up. Jonathan watched as his boy walked from chair to chair, as he gripped the edge of the cushions, then let go and landed heavily on his bottom. She'd made a motion for him to go to Jonathan, then stopped when Daniel turned and crawled back to her. She picked him up.

"He's been pulling himself up, letting go, and falling down a lot lately," Jonathan explained.

"He's doing it because he wants to walk unaided, Jonathan. That's what is important."

Jonathan wanted to tell Vivienne that *she* was important. More important to him than she could imagine. And he'd missed her since she'd returned to the ranch. Daniel couldn't talk yet he knew his son had also missed her. Daniel yawned and dropped his head on Vivienne's shoulder.

"It's almost bedtime for the birthday boy, because he took an abbreviated nap this afternoon," he murmured.

"If you don't mind, I'd like to give him a bath and put him to sleep."

Jonathan recalled what had happened the last time she'd given Daniel a bath. That he had been so turned on when seeing her body through her wet shirt that he'd had a problem falling and staying asleep when plagued by recurring erotic dreams of making love to Vivienne.

"Okay."

He didn't want to refuse her because once he returned to work his schedule would change, and he doubted whether either of them would be able to spend much time together. "Once he's asleep, would you like a cup of cappuccino?"

Vivienne gave him a long stare. "Isn't this how it began with us? You inviting me into your home and offering coffee?"

A half smile lifted a corner of Jonathan's mouth. "Yes. It does sound like a rerun."

"And my answer is the same. Yes."

Jonathan wanted to tell Vivienne that he needed a beverage a lot stronger than coffee. A couple of shots of bourbon would do the trick in dulling his senses, so he didn't have to acknowledge that he, Vivienne, and Daniel had become a family. The weeks had passed since Daniel had come home with him, and he was also expected to take over running and sharing Porter Oil with Imani. Deep down, he knew that with all those responsibilities it would be impossible for him to have a normal relationship with a woman. Even with someone as incredible as Vivienne Fortune, who had captured not only his heart, but also his son's. His plate was full to overflowing.

Call it instinct, or women's intuition. But Vivienne knew Jonathan wasn't the same man he'd been before she left to bathe and put Daniel to bed when she entered the kitchen. The expression on his face spoke volumes.

She knew for certain something was wrong when she hugged him and he went stiff. "When were you going to tell me?"

"Tell you what?"

"Please don't insult my intelligence by pretending you don't know what I'm talking about."

"All right. I can't a handle a relationship at this time in my life, Vivienne. Even in the past when I tried, but they never worked out for me. I knew I was falling in love with Daniel's mother, but it was something I never told her. And when she asked for a marriage proposal and I told her I wasn't ready for marriage she decided we were through. And because of that, I wasn't with her when she needed me the most."

Vivienne was trying to wrap her head around what Jonathan was telling her. "Why didn't you tell her you loved her?"

Jonathan shook his head. "I don't know. We hadn't dated that long and I still didn't trust her completely because I thought she was with me because I was a Porter. I suppose unconsciously I was comparing her to other women I'd dated, who soon as they heard the name *Porter*, they would see me as their personal ATM."

"But it's different for me because I don't want or need you for your money, Jonathan."

"Because you have money."

Vivienne was struggling not to break down. "And because I have money that makes me different from the other women you dated?"

"No."

"Then what *is* it, Jonathan?"

"I suck when it comes to relationships, and I can't do this," he gritted out.

"Yes, you can, if we do it together."

Jonathan closed his eyes as he shook his head. "You don't think I want it to work with us? I do. But…"

"But what, Jonathan?" she whispered.

He shook his head again. "I think it's best for you to go."

Vivienne knew he wasn't going to change his mind and

she wasn't going to beg or plead with him that they were meant for each other. Walking out of the kitchen, she gathered her bag, leaving Jonathan, Daniel, and her heart behind.

She felt like an automaton as she drove back to the ranch; she was determined not to cry. Vivienne had never shed tears in the past over a failed relationship, and she wasn't going to start now. However, she couldn't blink back the tears when she thought about Daniel. She loved the baby as if he'd come from her and Jonathan.

And it wasn't as if she didn't know Jonathan was still grieving the loss of the woman who'd given him a son. A woman with whom he'd fallen in love, and after their breakup had sacrificed her life to bring his child into the world. There was no way she could compete with a dead woman; not one with the power to control the father of her child from the grave.

Vivienne knew she'd surprised her mother when she called to tell her she'd planned to eat lunch with her when they'd shared dinner the night before. Although she tried to hide her heartache behind too-bright smiles, it was obvious she hadn't fooled her mother. Table conversation always segued, as usual, to who was the mastermind behind the thefts and the hope that whoever it was would eventually slip up.

Darla stopped her as she prepared to leave. "What's the matter with you, sweetie?"

Vivienne's mouth was smiling but her eyes weren't. "It has nothing to do with me," she lied smoothly. "It's about the Fortunes. I feel the family is under attack with that grifter demanding a half million dollars to sell her baby, and although Micah caught the man stealing from us, he's refused to say who'd hired him because he claims he was paid too well to snitch."

Darla angled her head. "Are you certain that's all it is?"

"Yes. What else could there be?" Vivienne asked.

"I don't know. You tell me."

"I'm going to tell you that I'm good, Mom." She pulled her mother into a tight hug. "But I have to leave now because Drake sent me a text. He wants me to stop by his office at three."

"Okay, sweetie. Love you."

"I love you, too."

It didn't take long for Vivienne to discover why Drake wanted to talk to her in person when he told her Rafe had heard from the front desk at the guest ranch that a man named Cameron Wells called to say he'd received a Gift of Fortune invitation. And he planned to come to the ranch next month for a week.

A frown furrowed Vivienne's forehead. "I don't remember seeing a nomination with his name. Maybe we missed it."

"I don't think so. Neither I nor Rafe sent him an invitation, and we never got a nomination for him. I have no idea how he'd obtained an invitation."

Vivienne sighed. "That's really weird." She paused. "What was his story that resulted in his winning the coveted invite?

Drake shook his head. "There was no story."

"So, you have no idea who he is or how he got ahold of the invitation?" Vivienne asked.

"Nope. But we will find out once he shows up next month with the invitation."

"I don't know about you, Drake, but I'm beginning to

feel that Emerald Ridge has entered an alternative universe with all that's been going on." The police had finally extracted DNA from all the ranch hands, and they had signed releases so the test can be done. So once again they were playing a waiting game.

"You're right. But meanwhile me and Rafe will try and get to the bottom of it."

Jonathan felt as if his well-ordered world was falling apart. He had only a few more days with Daniel before he had to return to his job at Porter Oil. Although he'd planned to set up a hybrid schedule, where he'd work remotely one or two days a week, it was incumbent that he return to the office on a full-time basis for the first month before revising his schedule.

He'd tried and failed not to think about Vivienne, unable to believe how she'd managed to become so much a part of his life in only a month. And it wasn't only in his life, but also Daniel's. Each time the doorbell rang his baby boy became alert as if he were waiting for Vivienne to walk through the door.

Jonathan was finally able to exhale two days later, when he received a text from Vivienne that she'd found a spot for Daniel at FGR day care, and he had to call the director to set up an appointment to come in for an orientation.

He stared at the text message with the realization that even though they weren't together, she still cared about his son. Daniel meant the world to Vivienne, and despite Jonathan's denials, he had fallen head over heels in love with her.

Had he made the worst mistake of his life letting her go?

He called his sister using FaceTime. "Hey, sis. I need some advice."

"Say what?" she drawled. "I can't believe you're asking me for advice."

He frowned. "I'm serious, Imani."

"Okay."

"I like Vivienne, but I don't know what to do about it."

"Like, Jonathan? Don't you mean you're *in love* with her?"

"Yes, I love her. And so does Daniel."

Shaking her head and blowing out her cheeks, Imani said, "Why the heck are you calling me when you should tell Vivienne how you feel about her? What you're trying to control is something you can't control. And that is love. You better go and tell her how you feel, then put a ring on her finger before another man sees what you see and decides to scoop her up for himself.

"That's not going to happen," he growled.

"Says who, Jonathan Porter?"

"Says me. I'll talk to you later."

He spent the next two hours pacing the floor and talking to himself as he contemplated how to make up with Vivienne. He'd called himself every unsavory name he could think of for sending her away when she'd said they could work out any problem they had—together.

And Imani was right. He was trying to control something that was impossible. He'd made a mistake not telling Danielle that he loved her, but there was no way he was going to make the same mistake twice.

He waited for Daniel to wake up from his nap. Picking up him, he kissed his forehead. "Baby boy, you and I need to take a ride." Jonathan, changed him, then packed a bag with a supply of diapers and several change of clothes. "Let's go, buddy. We're going to see Vivienne."

Chapter Sixteen

Jonathan was aware the Fortune's Gold Ranch was big, much too massive for him to find Vivienne's house. He drove slowly through the main gate and stopped at the main building and spa. It was where he'd come with Vivienne to drop off Daniel at day care when they'd gone to the jail to see the thief.

He took Daniel out of his child safety seat and carried him into the building. Jonathan did not intend on wasting time driving around looking for Vivienne, when all he had to do ask the concierge to contact her. He found the concierge's office and knocked lightly on the door to get his attention.

Philip Henley came to his feet and rounded his desk. "How may I help you?"

"I would like to meet with Vivienne Fortune, but I have no idea where to contact her."

"Miss Fortune is the forewoman of the cattle ranch."

"I'm aware of that, and it is very important that I talk to her in person."

The concierge affected a practiced professional smile. "I can call her. Whom should I say is asking for her?"

"Jonathan Porter."

Philip nodded like a bobblehead doll. "Yes, Mr. Porter. I

will call her right away." He returned to his desk and tapped buttons on the phone, speaking softly. The call lasted less than ten seconds. "She's on her way."

"Thank you for your help. I'll wait for her in the lobby."

The man smiled. "I'm glad I could be of assistance."

Jonathan, carrying Daniel, pressed his mouth to his son's hair. "It's about to begin, buddy. Either she's open to joining Team Porter, or she can decide she's better off without us."

He sat on a chair in the lobby, facing the entrance, and settled Daniel on his lap. The furnishings in the lobby were elegant and pleasing to the eye, and the perfect place to sit and while away the time in understated luxury.

Vivienne walked into the guest ranch lobby, her mind in tumult. When Philip had called to tell her Jonathan wanted to meet with her, every imaginable scenario went through her head. Had something happened to Daniel? Had he decided to go back to Dubai and live there permanently?

Her heart beat a double-time rhythm when her eyes fell on him where he stood, cradling Daniel to his chest. He was the Jonathan Porter she'd admired from afar so long ago. He'd exchanged his T-shirts and jeans for a tailored gray Western-style suit, matching Stetson, and highly polished black boots.

They were less than a hairbreadth away from each other when Daniel reached out for her to take him. "Hey, sweetie," she crooned, savoring the crush of his chubby body against her chest.

"Mum, mum, mum," Daniel said, as he patted her face.

Vivienne felt her eyes fill and she feared embarrassing herself, when Jonathan curved an arm around her waist. "Let's go back to your place, where we can talk."

Blinking back tears, she nodded. She didn't know if

Daniel was trying to say *mama,* but that no longer mattered because in that instant, she vowed to fight for Jonathan and Daniel with the same focus and energy she'd used to become forewoman of FGR. They went outside to the parking area, and she stopped at her pickup.

"We'll take my car," Jonathan said. "You can drive."

It stood to reason that Jonathan would want to take his car because of the child safety seat. After securing Daniel in his seat, Jonathan got into the Porsche beside her, the scent of his cologne wafting to her nostrils as she started the engine. Memories of their lovemaking came back as she drove to her house. It had become a time when they ceased to exist as separate entities and were one with the other.

She drove past the homes of her brothers and maneuvered into the driveway of a structure that was a smaller version of the mansion where she'd grown up. Vivienne shut off the engine, exited the SUV, and walked to the front door, leaving Jonathan to follow with Daniel. It was on a rare occasion that she used the front door because she didn't want to track grass and mud inside; she always left her boots in the mudroom at the rear of the house.

Jonathan stood in the middle of her family room. "I thought you told me you had a *little* place on the ranch."

Smiling, Vivienne met his eyes. "It is a little place when compared to the main house, where I grew up. And three thousand square feet is half the size of your humble abode," she teased, as she took Daniel from Jonathan and folded her body down to a love seat. Jonathan followed and he took a facing one. "What do you want to talk about?"

"Us," Jonathan replied.

"What about us, Jonathan?"

A beat passed. "I thought about what you said about us making it together."

She glared at him. When she'd asked—no, practically begged him to talk to her about their possibly having a future together, he'd dismissed her as if she were an annoyance.

She didn't beg then, and she had no intention of ever begging Jonathan to love her as much as she loved him.

Jonathan stared at the woman holding his son, recognizing why he'd fallen in love with her. She wasn't a spoiled rich girl expecting to get whatever she wanted. Vivienne Fortune was strong, confident, and independent. All the qualities he wanted in a life partner. And then there was Daniel. His son had become her Achilles heel because she had come to love him as much as he did. Even when he'd asked her to leave, there were no histrionics or tears. She'd walked out of his house and his life without looking back. However, it was different with Daniel. When he'd called her what sounded like *mama*, it was the first time Jonathan had witnessed her vulnerability.

"What about us, Jonathan?" Vivienne asked again.

"I love you."

Her lips parted when she smiled. "I know that."

Jonathan's eyebrows shot up. "You knew?"

"Of course, I knew. I always knew you were too proud and stubborn to admit it."

"So, you think you know me that well, hmm?"

"It's not what I think, Jonathan, but what I *know*. If you hadn't felt something for me, you wouldn't have trusted me to spend as much time with Daniel as you did because you're overly protective of him. I also knew for certain that you more than liked me the first time we slept together."

His eyes crinkled at the corners as he looked over at her. "You knew that, too?"

"Of course. And I knew that I was falling in love with you but decided that would remain my secret. Everything changed for me once I lived with you for several days. I hadn't known up until that time that I wanted more than a relationship."

"What do you want now, Vivienne?" Jonathan asked softly.

"I don't want to play make-believe house."

"You wouldn't have to if we were married."

She closed her eyes for several seconds. "Are you proposing to me, Jonathan Porter?"

He leaned forward. "Yes, I am, Vivienne Fortune. I'm asking if you would marry me, the three of us will become Team Porter and Fortune."

A rush of color suffused Vivienne's throat and face. "That's only going to happen if we become Team Fortune and Porter."

"Hell, woman. It doesn't matter what name comes first as long as we're a family."

Vivienne stood and gave Jonathan his son. "Please hold him while I get something."

Jonathan bounced Daniel on his knees while he waited for Vivienne's return. "I hope she's going to say yes," he whispered in the child's ear. He didn't have to wait long for Vivienne to come back and hand him the check he'd written to reimburse her for the items she'd purchased to decorate Daniel's nursery. "You didn't deposit it?"

"No! And I had no intention of depositing it. I told you what I bought was a gift and you weren't gracious enough to accept it as a gift. And I'm not going to accept your marriage proposal until you accept Daniel's gift."

Jonathan realized Vivienne was holding all the cards

in the deck and he didn't have another move. Grasping the check, he tore it in half. "Consider it done."

Smiling, Vivienne sat beside him. "Now, ask me again?"

"Miss Vivienne Fortune, will you do me the honor of becoming my wife and the mother of our son?"

"Why does it sound as if you've rehearsed this in advance?"

Jonathan settled Daniel on the chair, then went down on one knee. Reaching for Vivienne's hand, he kissed the back of it. "Miss Vivienne Fortune, the love of my life, will you please do me the honor of becoming my wife and the mother of our son?"

Throwing an arm around his neck, Vivienne kissed him, then Daniel's cheek. "Yes, and yes!"

"Now that you're my fiancée, it's time I put a ring on your finger. I don't know what you have on your work schedule, but I'd like for us to drive to Dallas where you can select a ring, and afterward, we celebrate at a restaurant of your choice."

"Sounds perfect!" She beamed up at him, her eyes glimmering with tears. "I'm going to call Drake and have him cover for me, then I'm going to shower and change into something suitable for a woman who has just accepted a marriage proposal from a man who unknowingly had stolen my heart a long time ago. And it took a thief to make my fantasy a reality."

Staring at Vivienne under lowered lids, he whispered, "I love you today, I'll love you tomorrow, and I'll love you forever."

Later that evening, the wing of Hayden and Darla's home was filled with Fortunes as Vivienne proudly showed off the three-carat Asscher-cut solitaire flanked by brilliant marquis diamonds on her left hand. Daniel appeared quite content in Darla's arms as she dropped light kisses on his curly hair.

Jonathan had driven to a high-end jeweler in Dallas, where she'd tried on several rings before selecting one. Daniel had slept during the ride and while she'd held him on her lap at the jewelry store, he'd woken up just as they pulled into the parking lot of a popular restaurant advertising some of the best steaks, brisket, and barbecue in the city. Jonathan had secured a table while she went to the restroom to change Daniel. After they'd given the server their food order, Vivienne had called her mother to inform her she was engaged to Jonathan Porter, and to get the entire family together later that evening for an impromptu celebration.

Hayden's flushed face was an indication that he'd had at least one, maybe two, celebratory shots of bourbon before everyone else. "I know everyone is as shocked as I am that my daughter is engaged to marry into one of Texas's finest families. The Porters."

"Don't you mean the richest," someone called out.

Hayden's expression grew serious. "You can't buy love. Right, baby girl?"

Vivienne moved closer to Jonathan, lacing their fingers together. "You're right, Dad. I'd marry Jonathan even if he didn't have a penny to his name. I love him just that much."

A grinning Hayden raised his glass. "To Jonathan and Vivienne." There was an echoing sentiment before everyone tossed back their drinks.

"Are you sure you want to become a member of this family?" she asked Jonathan wryly.

"Only if you're sure you want to become a Porter."

She brushed a kiss over his mouth. "I've never been surer of anything in my life."

"Get a room!" a chorus of voices said in unison.

Jonathan laughed. "I have plenty of room whenever you yokels want to stop by."

"What about tomorrow?" Drake asked.

Vivienne squinted at her brother. "It's best you call before you come, or you'll get to see something that just might embarrass you." She'd agreed to move out of her house on the ranch to live with Jonathan. She'd also told him she wanted to wait until after they were married to try to give Daniel a little sister or brother.

"Your mother seems quite taken with Daniel, and he with her," Jonathan remarked.

"That's because she wants grandchildren. There's no doubt the two of them will get along very well together, and she said she's always available if we need a babysitter."

"Between the Fortunes in Emerald Ridge and the Porters in Chatelaine, we won't have a problem with finding a babysitter for Daniel."

"I hope that isn't too often, Jonathan. I want Daniel to know his mother before handing him off to others, even if they are family." The moment she'd accepted Jonathan's marriage proposal, she had become Daniel's mother and he, her son.

Vivienne had almost given up finding love, yet it had found her with Jonathan and Daniel Porter.

* * * * *